9

A GILBERT MORRIS MYSTERY

MOODY PRESS
CHICAGO

© 2000 by
GILBERT MORRIS

ISBN: 0-8024-4033-9

1 3 5 7 9 10 8 6 4 2

Printed in the United States of America

Contents

The House on Barber Road

Will you girls hurry up! The way you're riding those bikes, it'll take us a year and a day to get anywhere."

But Juliet saw her brother grinning as he glanced back at her and her friend Jenny White. Gleams from the late afternoon sun caught Joe's red hair, and his blue eyes looked full of fun.

The two girls pedaled harder to make it up the steepest hill on Barber Road.

Juliet Jones, at the age of ten, was one year older than Joe, but she never had been able to equal him on a bicycle. Though she was strong for a girl, her brother was extrastrong for his age. And that made a big difference when riding a bike.

"You just wait for us, Joe!" she panted, pumping as hard as she could. "Wait for us at the top."

"Well, Too Smart Jones," Jenny White gasped, "you may solve mysteries, but you sure can't ride a bike as fast as Joe can."

"Don't call me Too Smart!" Juliet snapped back. She was almost out of breath. She hated to be called by that nickname. It had come about because she was intelligent, she loved to study, and she got good grades. In fact, she got better grades than most of her friends. That was why somebody had started calling her "Too Smart Jones" way back when she was going to public school.

Jenny White was nine. She also had reddish hair, and her blue eyes were large and expressive and pretty. She was wearing a pair of faded jeans today and a white T-shirt with a picture of a lion on the front.

At the top of the hill, Joe wheeled to a stop and waited until the girls caught up with him. When they got there, both breathing hard, he just grinned at them broadly. "You're going to have to get in shape. You two are getting fat."

"I am not fat!" Juliet yelped. She knew she wasn't fat. In fact, she thought she was very trim looking in her lime green T-shirt and white shorts.

"Look at that big old place over there," Jenny said, pointing off to their right. "I always think it looks spooky."

Juliet and Joe looked.

The house was three stories high. It was

made of gray stone, and green ivy grew up its sides. The two tall spires on the roof reached into the sky like the steeples on a church.

"I never paid any attention to that house," Joe said with a shrug.

"It's set so far back off the road that you hardly know it's there," Juliet said. "You can go right by out here on the road and never see it. Of course, we don't go up this road a lot, anyway."

The three kept looking at the gloomy old house while they caught their breath.

"The place looks sort of like a church," Joe murmured. "With those steeples on top and all."

"I'm glad we *don't* come this way a lot," Jenny put in. "I've heard that house is haunted."

Juliet sniffed. "Don't be silly! There's no such thing as a haunted house, Jenny."

"That's what people say, anyhow."

"I've heard stories about the place, now that I think of it," Joe said. "I remember noticing it one time, but it was a cloudy day, and I couldn't see it this good."

Jenny reached into her backpack and took out an apple. She took a bite and held it out to Juliet. "Want a bite?"

"No, thanks." Juliet was still staring at the house. "I wonder why people would think it's haunted."

"Hey, give me a bite!" Joe was always interested in food. He snatched the apple from Jenny's hand, took an enormous bite, and then handed it back.

"You took half of my apple!" she cried. "Oh, just keep it. I have another one." She took another apple from her backpack and chewed on a bite, looking thoughtful. "They say it's haunted because nobody's lived there for a long time, and there was something funny about the people that built it. That's what people say."

"What do you mean something funny? Did they tell jokes or something?" Joe laughed loudly at his own try at humor.

"Oh, not that kind of funny!" Jenny shook her head, sending her reddish curls bobbing violently. "I mean they acted funny. Peculiar. The house used to belong to a family called Norworthy. My grandma used to tell me about them. Different members of the family just started disappearing without a trace. Nobody ever knew where they went."

Juliet at once turned from the house and fixed her eyes on Jenny. "Disappearing. You mean just . . . vanishing?"

"Now wait a minute, Juliet. Don't start trying to make a mystery out of this." Jenny was laughing at her.

As a matter of fact, Juliet did have a habit of seeing mysteries. Besides, she had even solved several of them. Some people called her

Sherlock after the great British detective Sherlock Holmes.

"You'd better watch out, Jenny," Joe warned, holding up both hands. "She'll get you into investigating with her."

"Don't be silly!" Juliet said, scowling at him. "When people disappear, I just think it's . . . it's unusual."

The sky had grown darker, and strands of gray clouds began drifting overhead. Jenny looked nervous, and then she shivered. "Anyway, the place looks kind of spooky to me. I don't like it."

Joe shrugged his shoulders again. "Looks OK to me. Let's go up the lane and take a look."

"We can't do that," Jenny protested. "It's somebody else's property."

"Sure we can. Come on. We can at least look in the windows and see what we can see."

Juliet said, "It won't hurt to just look. Come on, Jenny, don't be a fraidy-cat."

"I'm not a fraidy-cat," Jenny said. She was obviously scared, though, and when they were halfway up the weedy lane to the house, she said, "I just don't think we ought to go poking around. I'm going to stop right here, and you two better not go closer, either."

"You can be the rear guard, then," Joe told her with a laugh. "Let's go, Juliet."

Juliet and Joe followed the lane up to the

old mansion. They laid down their bikes at the bottom of the high steps that reached up to a large porch.

"Let's go up," Joe said. If he was nervous about being so close to a haunted house, he did not tell Juliet.

By now she was feeling a little nervous herself. But she never liked Joe to think that she was afraid of anything. So she followed him up the rickety steps to the porch.

First, they tried to peer in a window but could see nothing.

"It looks like all the windows are covered with heavy drapes," Juliet said.

"Let's try the door."

Juliet opened her mouth to protest.

But before she could get words out, Joe had already stepped up to the big front door. He turned the knob and gave the door a push.

"Somebody forgot to lock it," he whispered.

"What are you whispering about?" Juliet asked. "And shut that door. This is somebody else's house."

"I don't know why I whispered," he said. He pushed the door farther open, and it squeaked.

"It even sounds like the door of a haunted house," he said.

"Don't talk about haunted houses!" Juliet gave him a mean look. "And shut the door!"

But Joe pushed the door open farther still, peeked in, and proceeded to walk into the house.

Without another thought, Juliet followed close on his heels.

What she saw right away was a big, gloomy entryway. Looking up and around, she said, "This has got to be the biggest front hall I've ever seen."

"It sure is," Joe said. "And look at the two winding staircases."

"It's almost like Tara."

"What's Tara?"

"That house in *Gone with the Wind*. I saw it on TV."

The windows were indeed draped, but enough light came in around the edges for Juliet to see that what furniture had been left was covered with white cloths.

Joe said, "I want to look upstairs."

"We'd better not. We don't belong in here." She knew what their parents would say.

"Oh, come on! There's nothing wrong with going upstairs. Nobody lives here. And we're just going to look."

Actually, Juliet was intensely curious herself. What was up there? "All right," she said, closing her ears to the little warning voice of her conscience.

"I'll take the left stairway, and you take the right one."

"OK." Juliet started up.

Since both stairways curved around, Juliet and Joe met on the balcony at the top and stood looking down at the entrance beneath them.

Then Juliet noticed the thick layer of dust on the balcony floor. She moved her foot through it, scraping the dust away. Then she cried, "Oh, see, Joe! There's a pretty marble floor."

He looked down. "This must have been some rich man's house."

"It's big and beautiful, but nobody's lived in it for a long time. I wonder why." Juliet smelled a mystery.

"Let's look in some of the rooms up here."

"OK," Juliet said, "but it'll be too dark to see much pretty soon."

At that moment a sudden noise sounded from somewhere over their heads—as though something heavy had been dropped. The house had been so still that both of them jumped and stared upward.

"Let's get going!" Joe whispered. "Somebody's in here."

"We'd better. And quick." Juliet raced after him down the stairs, and they dashed out of the house. Then they started running.

When they got to the place where Jenny was waiting, she gaped at them. "What's the matter? What *happened* in there?" she cried.

"Let's just get out of here," Joe said hoarsely.

He jumped on his bike and began pedaling without another word.

The girls got on theirs, and the three of them barreled down the weedy lane to Barber Road.

Juliet took a quick look over her shoulder at the house, and she gasped.

"A light!" she cried out. "There's a light way up on the top floor!"

Joe and Jenny did not stop pedaling, but they both glanced back.

"I don't see any light," Joe said and kept going.

"I don't either."

"Well, it was there."

Juliet looked back again. "It's gone now, but I saw it. I know I saw it."

Jenny just pedaled hard, looking straight ahead. "Maybe you just thought you saw one."

Juliet did not argue, but she knew she was right. She *had* seen a light. They kept going, getting farther and farther away from the scary house. "Even if my eyes were playing a trick on me," she muttered, "what about that noise? *Something* was up there."

Her mind began racing. *Maybe it was a cat knocking over something that we heard. No, it couldn't have been a cat, because a cat can't turn on a light—and I know I saw a light.*

They kept wheeling along, for dark would be falling soon. Juliet could not get her mind off the house. She said, "People think it's haunted, but there's no such thing as a haunted house!" Still, she could not help thinking of how strange the place was. She thought of the light and the noise upstairs. Something weird was going on at the Barber Road Mansion.

When Juliet and Joe reached home, they put their bicycles away, then stood talking for a while before going in.

"What are we going to do about all this stuff?" he asked.

"I haven't the faintest idea what you're talking about."

Joe grinned at her, knowingly. "Don't you think I know you, sister dear? I know what you're thinking."

"I don't know myself what I'm thinking."

"You are thinking," Joe said, "of how you can solve this great mystery of the haunted house. You always think like that."

"I do not!"

"Do too!"

Juliet turned up her nose and started up the back steps. "You're just talking, Joe."

"Yeah? Then, let me ask you this—are you going to tell Mom and Dad where we were? Are you?"

Juliet stopped on the porch and stood dead-still. She turned to stare at Joe. "I—I don't think they'd be interested."

He laughed out loud. "You know you don't

mean that. They *would* be interested. What you mean is you don't want them to know."

"I don't want them to worry."

"That's what you always say when you want to keep something from them."

Juliet gave Joe a hard look, then walked into the house. She found her mother working at the stove.

"Hello," Mrs. Jones said. "Supper's close to being ready. Did you have a good time?"

"Oh, sure," Juliet said, glancing at Joe and hoping he would keep still. "We've been riding most of the time."

"Bicycle riding is good for your health," Joe said importantly. "All the doctors say so."

"That's right. They do. Now, go get cleaned up for supper. I'll be calling you soon."

"OK, Mom. Be right back." Joe darted toward the stairs.

When Juliet lingered, her mother looked up from the stove and asked, "Something wrong, Juliet?"

"Oh, not really."

"You're not sick or anything?"

"No, ma'am."

"Worried about your schoolwork?"

"Oh, no, Mom!"

"No reason to. You never fall behind."

Juliet started to leave, then turned back to say, "I'll help you with supper when I get my hands washed, Mom."

"Oh, it's just a roast. Everything's about done, but thanks."

"Then I'll do the dishes after."

"That would be a help."

Juliet still hesitated, but finally she started upstairs. She found Joe waiting for her at the top.

"Did you tell her?"

"Tell her what?"

"That we've been out looking for ghosts in a haunted house."

"Oh, that's silly!"

"Is it?"

Juliet sniffed and sailed by him, saying, "You know we weren't doing that."

She closed the door to her room. What she was doing about their afternoon adventure troubled her. Maybe she would tell her parents about the haunted house after all—but not today.

"Mrow!"

Looking down, she saw Boots. The black kitten rubbed around her ankles. Juliet scooped up the cat and whispered, "Boots, I think I like mysteries too much."

"Mrow!"

"Can't you say anything but *mrow?*" Juliet stroked him. She loved her cat. Then she put him down to wash her hands and headed for the bathroom.

When she came back to her room, she began to quickly brush her hair.

"Mrow!"

"You again!"

She picked up Boots just as a knock came at her door and Joe stuck his head in. "Hi. What about if I come in?"

"What for?"

"Just to talk. Mom's going to call us anytime now."

"Oh, all right. Come on."

Joe stepped into Juliet's room. "Boy, I'd sure like to go back to that house." His voice rang with excitement.

Juliet looked at him. "I'm not sure we should."

But her brother said, "Well, *I'm* going back."

Their mother called them just then, and Joe turned to go downstairs. Then he looked back and grinned knowingly. "You won't be able to stay away!"

2

The Strange Car

With a sigh, Too Smart Jones closed her history book and sat back in her chair. She rubbed her eyes and then reached for the can of Diet Coke on her desk. Looking around the room idly, she thought, *I must have spent years in this room.*

As a matter of fact, since it was her schoolroom, she did spend a great deal of time there. Juliet and her brother were homeschooled by their mother.

Their father had made them a fine schoolroom upstairs. There were maps on the walls, a huge globe sitting on a table over to one side, and two desks placed so that they provided private work space. A computer sat in one corner.

The room did seem rather cluttered because of all the old projects on display. Joe thought he was an inventor, and several of his inventions sat here and there. There was an alarm system—though not in use. Just touching one of the windows of the Jones house would set off the alarm. Unfortunately, it was so sensitive that even the touch of a squirrel's paw or the blowing breeze would sometimes set it off. Nevertheless Joe was proud of it, as he was of the rest of his projects.

Juliet's area was covered with books, instead. She loved to read, and that helped her to be good at her studies.

The only trouble she had was with the librarian, Mrs. Ida Smathers. Mrs. Smathers was a tall, thin woman who didn't like people to check out books from her library. "It makes gaps in the shelves," she said.

Many were the battles that Juliet fought with Mrs. Smathers. Once in a while Juliet liked to check out a book that was written for grownups. Mrs. Smathers thought that was not a good idea.

Juliet thought of the librarian and snorted. "She wants me to read Dick and Jane for the rest of my life, I suppose."

Juliet was still sitting there, now lazily wondering where Joe was, when suddenly the door burst open and he came flying in with a box in his hand.

"Joe, you never enter a room like a normal

person," she complained. "You come in like a tornado."

"That's because I'm a very dramatic person," he said.

"No, you're just bad mannered."

"Aw, that's not so."

"You're uncouth."

"I'm as couth as you are!"

"There's no such word as *couth*."

"Why isn't there? If some people are uncouth, some people have to be couth."

"*Uncouth* is a word, but *couth* isn't. I thought you knew that."

"Oh, come on!'

"It's true!"

"Well, *couth* is a word now—I just used it."

"You can't go around making up words!"

"Why can't I?"

Juliet rolled her eyes. "What do you want, Joe?"

"I'll bet you're going to love what I've done now."

"What have you done?" Juliet asked without much curiosity. "Have you invented a perpetual motion machine?"

"Better than that," Joe said. "Just look at this."

Joe opened his box. Then he took out a strange looking object. It appeared to be a cross between eyeglasses and binoculars.

"What in the world is that?"

"It's my newest invention. It's a pair of night vision goggles."

"You couldn't make anything like that!" Juliet said with disbelief.

"Yes, I could. I got the basic thing from the army surplus store, and then I improved on it. And I made two pairs of them. Here. Try out one."

Juliet picked up a pair of Joe's goggles. They seemed very heavy. "These would break a person's neck."

"They've got to be heavy because they run on batteries," Joe explained.

Juliet put on the glasses and stared through them. The tight straps hurt her head. She looked all around and said, "What good are they? I can't see much of anything."

"Of course, you can't. It's not dark. But you just wait till it gets dark, and then you'll see."

When Juliet heard that, she grew interested at once. "These could be kind of fun—if they work."

"Oh, they'll work all right. The man at the store said they would. They had a broken part and were in pretty bad shape, so I got 'em for ten dollars apiece. You owe me ten dollars for yours."

"I don't have that much money to give you."

"Oh. Well . . . you don't have to, then. I'll sell 'em to Billy Rollins. I'll charge him twenty dollars for them, though."

"No, no. I'll buy them if they work," Juliet said. "I'll save up and pay you."

"OK, then. We'll go try them tonight."

They started to talk about what things a person might do with the glasses like these.

And then the door opened, and in came their mother. Mrs. Jones was a pretty woman with reddish brown hair and brown eyes. She came over and ruffled Joe's hair, saying, "What are you two up to?"

"Oh, nothing much."

Juliet hid a smile. She suspected that Joe didn't want to tell their mother how much of his spending money he had used to buy the night glasses.

He added quickly, "Juliet's probably going to solve another mystery."

She glared at him.

Mrs. Jones sighed. "Another mystery. Don't you ever get tired of mysteries, Juliet? What is it this time?"

"Oh, it's nothing, Mom!" Juliet saw that Joe was about to go into the subject of the haunted house, and she wanted to head that off. It would be better if he didn't, she thought. Not yet. "Mom, is it OK if Joe and I bike downtown for a while—since we're done with school stuff?"

"I suppose so."

"And then I'd like to go over to the Del Rios' and play with Delores for a while."

"Yeah, Samuel and I could do some stuff, too," Joe put in.

Samuel and Delores Del Rio were good friends of Juliet and Joe's. They lived with their grandparents in an interesting old house, and nothing pleased Juliet and her brother much more than spending an afternoon over there. Mrs. Del Rio would always feed them some delicious Mexican food.

"You may do that too, but don't be late for supper."

"Mom," Joe promised firmly, "you can count on that."

"I'll bet I can." She gave a laugh as they both got up, ready to fly out of the schoolroom. "You may forget a lot of things, but as far as I know you've never forgotten a meal."

Thirty minutes later Juliet and Joe were sitting in the ice cream shop. Joe had gotten a rocky road, and Juliet was eating her favorite, pistachio.

Delores and Sam Del Rio sat in the booth across from them. Both had olive skin, glossy black hair, and dark brown eyes. And both of the Del Rio children were acrobats. Their father and mother had been aerialists with the circus, and they had taught them. Now Delores and Sam lived with their grandfather and grandmother, who also had been aerialists in a circus. So Delores and Samuel could do backflips and all other kinds of wonderful gymnastic tricks.

"I don't see how you eat that stuff, Delores," Joe said suddenly. "This is an ice cream shop. Why don't you get real ice cream?"

"Because I like this better." Delores took another spoonful of her strawberry sherbet. "Besides, ice cream will make you fat if you eat enough of it."

"Then let me be fat," Sam said. His curly hair was falling down over his forehead as he spooned black walnut ice cream into his mouth. He stopped suddenly and grabbed at his head. "Ow!" he yelped. "That gave me a headache!"

"That's just because you eat it too fast, Sam," Delores told him.

"It's so good I can't help eating it fast," Sam said, still holding his head. "Besides, good ice cream's worth a little headache."

And then Delores looked across the table and asked brightly, "What have you two been doing?"

Before Juliet could stop him, Joe said, "We've been exploring a haunted house."

"A haunted house!" Sam took his hands from his head and gaped at Joe. "You're kidding me! What haunted house?"

"I'm not kidding. It's that old gray stone house with the two steeples on it—out west of town. On Barber Road."

"Sure. I know that place." Sam nodded his head. "It looks like a haunted house all right."

"Oh, there's no such thing as a haunted house," Juliet said.

"Yeah?" Joe smiled a knowing smile. "Seems to me you tore out of there quick enough when the ghost made a racket upstairs."

"A ghost! Really? Did you really see a *ghost?*" Delores gasped.

"No, we didn't see any ghost. He's just talking."

"You know there was something up there. We heard it—*you* heard it—and you said you saw a light when we were getting away from there."

"What kind of a light?" Sam asked.

Juliet thought it would be wise to get the subject changed. She glanced out the ice cream shop window and, fortunately, saw something interesting. She said, "Take a look at that!"

The others turned to the window.

Joe said, "I never saw a car like *that* in this town."

"That's a limousine," Sam said importantly. "They call them stretch limos. I've seen them in the movies."

Indeed, it was a long black car, much longer than an ordinary car. The windows were tinted too, so that it was impossible to see who was inside.

"Come on," Juliet said, getting up. "We've finished our ice cream." She hurried outside and watched the big car move slowly down the street. "I hope they stop and the people get out. I'd like to see who's in there," she murmured.

But the limo did not stop. And suddenly Juliet's sense of adventure rose in her. "Why don't we follow them and see where they go? They can't go very fast," she said. "Not in town."

"You can't keep up with a limo!" Joe protested.

But when Juliet jumped on her bike, the others got onto theirs and began to pedal.

Juliet had the strangest feeling about the black limousine. No car like that *ever* came to Oakwood. Seeing it here on their main street seemed so mysterious.

They pedaled furiously. But when they got to the edge of town, she saw it was hopeless. She watched the car speed up and then disappear.

"Well, that's that," Juliet said. She turned to the Del Rios. "Let's go over to your house and play."

"Sounds good to me," Sam said. "Let's have a race."

The girls let the boys do the racing, while they rode in a leisurely fashion to the Del Rio house.

First, nice old Mrs. Del Rio gave them quesa-
dillas for snacks. Afterward, the girls played in
the attic, where there were many old dresses and
hats and shoes. They loved to play dress up.

Joe and Samuel went off to pitch horse-
shoes—a game in which Joe was practically a
champion—until Juliet went outside and ended
their match. "Time to go home, Joe. You know
what Mom said about supper."

"OK. I guess I've beaten Sam enough for
one day." He clapped Sam on the shoulder.

"Just you wait until next time," Sam said.
"We'll practice turning backflips, and we'll see
who's the best at that."

"You always say that."

"Because it's always true!"

"Let's do some right now!"

"No, I'm tired of winning," Sam teased.
Then he grinned at Juliet. "Does he ever win at
anything?"

"Sure," Juliet said. "He wins at all the eating contests."

"I've got a natural talent for eating contests," Joe said. "Let's just find some food, and
we'll see who wins."

Sam said, "Let's play checkers next time. I
know I can win at that!"

Much of that evening, Juliet was unusual-
ly quiet. Mostly, she was wondering about the
strange, uncomfortable feeling she'd had when

they were in the gray stone mansion. She didn't like to call the place haunted, because she didn't believe in ghosts and witches. What especially troubled her was that she had had the same feeling when the black limousine had passed through town.

Why is that, I wonder? she asked herself. Just before bedtime, she took out her notebook and jotted down the events of the day. She liked to keep a record of all of her activities.

"I don't know why I feel so funny about that house," she wrote. "I don't believe in haunted houses, but the place just gave me an odd feeling. And then when that black car passed by, it looked—well, I guess 'sinister' is the best word to describe it. Or maybe just scary. Maybe it was because you couldn't see in. The windows were tinted, and there could have been anybody in there. Anyway, I'm going to keep an eye on things. There might be a mystery in this for me to work on."

She read over what she had written, then added: "I wish all I had to do was solve mysteries."

Juliet put away her journal, then brushed her hair, and lay down to read for a while. She was reading a book that asked the question, "What would Jesus do?"

But after a while Too Smart Jones grew too sleepy to read. She marked her place and turned out the light.

3

The Secret

Juliet Jones loved being homeschooled. One thing both she and her brother especially liked was that the Oakwood families who homeschooled their children got together every month in a Support Group meeting. When this happened, usually the parents met in the recreation room of a local church, while the boys and girls got to play outside.

It was a Wednesday afternoon, and the Oakwood Support Group was meeting. The younger children were on the playground, being supervised by two of the parents. But the older students were over to one side, playing basketball.

The strangest thing about their basketball game was that one of the players, Flash Gordon, was in a wheelchair. Juliet was on Flash's side, and she tossed the ball to him.

Flash arched his back, cradled the ball, and an instant later sent it flying into the air. It swished through the hoop without touching the rim.

"Yeah, Flash, great shot!" Juliet hollered.

Flash Gordon wheeled his chair around, making it spin. He said, "We've got these guys beat, Juliet. Just feed me that ball."

Juliet liked Flash. The boy was always cheerful. And he was always saying that God was going to heal his legs so that he could walk again someday.

She glanced around at some of the other players.

Chili Williams was probably the best all-around basketball player of them all. He was strong and quick. He also had large ears that stuck out from his head. He loved chili for every meal—including breakfast—which accounted for his nickname. His real name was Roy, but hardly anyone except his parents ever called him that.

Billy Rollins, at the age of ten, was an overweight boy. He was from a wealthy family, and Billy, to be truthful, was spoiled to the bone. He constantly bragged about the expensive toys and games that he had. He was talking to Ray and Helen Boyd, both also ten, who were on his team. They came from a well-to-do family as well, and the three of them had formed their own little group.

"Come on, Ray, let's show 'em how it's done!" Billy Rollins yelled.

Ray tossed the basketball to him, and Billy began dribbling down the dirt court. He should have passed the ball off to Jack Tanner or another player, but Billy was such a show-off that he usually tried to make the basket himself. This time he failed.

Flash wheeled his chair around quickly, and, unable to stop, Billy barreled into it. The ball went bouncing on. It was picked up by Chili, who tossed it to Juliet.

She took off dribbling toward the basket, as Helen tried to guard her. But out of the corner of her eye, Juliet could see what was happening across the court.

Billy had fallen onto Flash's lap. He was yelling, "Let me off of here! Let me off!"

"What's he doing to you, Billy?" Juliet called, dribbling and watching at the same time. "Looks to me like you're just getting a free ride."

Then Flash started spinning his wheelchair around and around. The chair was just a bright, metallic blur until, unexpectedly, Flash grabbed the wheels, stopped it, and Billy Rollins went flying off. He rolled along the court and got up with his face red, just as Juliet scored a basket.

"Great job, Juliet!" Flash said. "Great job, Billy! I never saw anybody roll as well as you do."

"Look at the dirt on my pants! You spoiled my best pair of pants!" Billy cried.

"Sorry about that, Billy. That's the way the cookie crumbles."

"These pants cost a lot of money!"

"They'll wash. And you almost knocked me out of my wheelchair. Was *that* good?"

"I'm going to tell my father."

"Tell the police too. Isn't there a crime called getting dirt on pants?"

They went back to playing, and Juliet's team won without any trouble. When the game broke up, the youngsters started playing shuffleboard, a game Juliet did not particularly like. Instead of playing, she wandered around to the swings.

She began to swing, then to pump herself higher and higher. Soon the swing was going as high as it could. It gave a little jump as it reached the highest point. Juliet thought, *I wonder if I could swing all the way over the top if I tried. I'll bet Samuel or Delores could—they're such good acrobats.*

She decided she had better not try that and gradually slowed down. Back and forth, back and forth she swung, beginning to think again of the haunted house.

Maybe I'll go back there when there's more daylight, she thought. *Then I can go in and get a better look.* She would ask Joe to go along. But then she thought, *No, Joe talks too much.*

36

I'll have to go alone. I want to keep this a secret for a while.

She happened to be coming downward on the swing just then, and at that moment someone gave her a tremendous shove. She let out a little scream, went sailing high, and almost fell off. As she swung back, she saw Jenny and Delores laughing up at her.

"Surprised you that time, didn't we?" Delores asked cheerfully.

Jenny, however, stopped laughing. She took hold of the swing rope and stopped it. "What's wrong with you today, Juliet?"

"What do you mean what's wrong with me today? Nothing's wrong with me today."

"Sure there is. Every time you get to thinking hard about something, you go off by yourself like this. You couldn't even keep your mind on the basketball game. What is it this time?"

"It's . . . nothing," Juliet said slowly. "It's really nothing."

"You think awfully hard about nothing," Delores commented.

"I know it," Juliet said. "It makes me mad the way that I waste time thinking about nothing."

Jenny said, "You sure do have a funny mind. Smart as you are, you sit around thinking about nothing!"

Then all three girls began to swing.

They had been pumping up and down together for several minutes when Jenny cried, "Oh, look at the parade!"

Juliet looked toward the street, and her heart seemed to leap into her throat.

Three large, important looking black cars were driving slowly by the church. Like the limo that she had seen before, all three had tinted windows, and she could not see a thing inside.

"They're going out toward Barber Road," Juliet murmured thoughtfully as she swung. "The same way that limo went the other day." Her mind began working quickly.

But right then Mrs. Tanner put her head out the church's back door to call, "All right, now. Everyone come back inside. It's time to do some work."

Most of the youngsters groaned. Playing was more fun than working, Joe often put it. But they trooped inside anyway.

When everyone was settled down, Mr. Tanner stood in front of the group.

Juliet liked Mr. Tanner. He had married Jenny White's mother, who was a widow. Mr. Tanner had one boy, named Jack, and now they lived together in a white frame house not far from where the Joneses lived.

"We have a new school project to announce," Mr. Tanner said with a smile. "I know you're going to like this one."

"Why don't we do a project testing the effect of ice cream on boys and girls?" Joe called out. Anybody could tell that he was trying to be funny. "I could be the specialist in chocolate."

"Yeah, and I could do strawberry," Chili said. His parents frowned at him. "Now you just keep quiet, son," Mr. Williams said. He was a tall, strong man. He was both a bricklayer and a deacon in the church.

"But, Dad, it's important to know what ice cream does to the human body," Chili said.

"Never you mind that. You just listen to Mr. Tanner."

"We'll have to put off the ice cream experiment for a while," Mr. Tanner said. "What we're going to do this time is a little volunteer work for the town."

"Work! We do enough work with our books," Billy Rollins grumbled. "What I need is a rest."

"I don't think this work will hurt you, Billy," Mr. Tanner said good-naturedly. "What we're going to do is clean up the litter alongside some of the roads just outside of town."

A groan went up from all directions.

Juliet whispered to Jenny, "I don't see that *that's* very educational."

"I didn't either, when Dad told me we were going to do it. I tried to talk him out of it, but he says it's good to help the town."

39

As soon as the meeting was over, Billy Rollins said in a loud voice, "*I'm* not going to pick up any garbage. My dad will hire a truck and a man to go by and do the work for me."

Unfortunately for Billy, his father was close enough to hear what he said. His face grew red, and he went straight to Billy. "I wouldn't think of spoiling this for you, Billy. Work is an opportunity. A lot of people in this world don't have jobs. They'd be glad to do a little work like this."

Billy began protesting to his father but did not seem to be getting anywhere. Juliet turned away. Other Support Group parents and children were talking and laughing together. Finally the crowd broke up, and everyone left for home.

As Juliet and Joe walked along behind their mom and dad, Juliet whispered, "Joe, don't you tell *anyone* about snooping in that old house."

"Of course I won't."

"Well, you almost did that one time. I don't think you would, but I thought I ought to warn you."

They kept on whispering and lagging behind for so long that Mrs. Jones looked back at them. "Come on along, you two. What are you whispering about?"

"Oh, nothing. We were just talking—and thinking," Juliet said quickly.

Their parents stopped and waited for them to catch up. Then without warning Mr. Jones picked up Juliet and tossed her in the air. He was very strong and did it so easily that she might as well have been stuffed with Ping-Pong balls. "When my girl starts thinking, I get worried." He often said that. Now he gave her a hug. "You be good now—like me."

Juliet found herself feeling very guilty. She glanced over at Joe and sighed. "Well, it's just that Joe and I were talking about that big gray house with the two sort of steeples out on Barber Road."

"Oh, that's the old Norworthy place! It must have been a fine old home in its time," Mr. Jones said.

"Well, Jenny said some people say it's haunted," Juliet told him. Her dad chuckled. "There was supposed to be a haunted house in every town I've ever lived in. And you know what? Every one of them turned out to be just an old house that was falling into ruin."

"Well, the Norworthy house isn't really falling into ruin," Mrs. Jones said. "Not yet. It was a fine home in its day and still is. I've often wondered why the owners don't just sell it. I believe it could be fixed up to be very nice again."

"Probably. But I have no idea where the owners are. I never knew them," Mr. Jones said. "Now let's get home, family. What are we having for supper tonight?"

"Your favorite." Mrs. Jones smiled a sneaky smile.

"Oh, you mean T-bone steaks and baked potatoes?"

"No. I mean leftover spaghetti and Texas toast."

Both Juliet and Joe howled, for they knew that this was not their father's favorite. But Juliet liked it, so she was happy. As the Joneses continued down the sidewalk toward home, she whispered to Joe, "I hate keeping secrets from the folks. Even for a while."

"Must not bother you too much." He gave her a lopsided grin. "You're always doing it."

This hurt Juliet's feelings, but then she realized there was some truth in what he said. She consoled herself by saying, "Well, we went just one time, and what we did really wasn't so bad, was it?" But to be honest with herself, she thought, *I am going to make one more visit tomorrow, though, just to be sure that there's nothing really there.*

4

The Window

Juliet cut up her waffle and buried it between strawberries. Then she topped it off with whipped cream.

Joe gave her one of his long looks. "You're always talking about the way *I* eat. The way you eat waffles looks to me like *you're* the pig in the family."

"I can't help it," Juliet said. "They're so good, Mom. You make the best breakfast in the world."

"That's no excuse for eating like that," Joe protested.

"You should talk!"

"I *am* talking!"

"Well, you should stop talking."

Mrs. Jones smiled. "You can say all the nice things about my breakfasts that you want, Juliet, but you're *not* getting another waffle. One of those is enough for anyone."

Juliet's mouth was full, but she mumbled, "Aw, Mom, I wasn't trying to get another one. I was just trying to be polite and tell you how good your cooking is."

Mr. Jones cleared his throat. "I do think you're right, Mother. Juliet doesn't need another waffle. But since I'm more than twice as large as she is, I'd better have two."

Joe howled at that. "You're always saying that when you want to do something, Dad. Especially when you want more dessert."

"There have to be some advantages to being grown up," Mr. Jones replied. "Besides, I have to work hard all day, and you kids just sit around and have a good time."

"I think you're not the only one who works," Mrs. Jones said. "I do a few things around the house."

"And I work like a dog!" Joe declared.

Juliet swallowed her piece of waffle. "Just having a good time? Loafing around? Dad, you know that's not so."

Mr. Jones never cracked a smile. He looked at their mother. "Have they been working, and I didn't know about it?"

"Come on, Dad," Joe said. "You know we work hard."

Mr. Jones sat back in his chair. "I know you do, son. I was just kidding. Well, in any case,

I've got to finish that bridge out north of town, so I'll need lots of energy. Another waffle, please, wife."

After breakfast, Too Smart Jones helped her mother clean up the kitchen, while Joe did some of his chores. Then Juliet dashed upstairs and was working hard at her desk by the time Joe came in. He saw what she was doing, then shook his head as he plopped down in his chair. "You working? I never saw anybody that liked schoolwork as much as Too Smart Jones. This is going overboard."

Juliet did not even look up. She did love schoolwork, and she was having fun learning some new math stuff.

Joe turned on the CD player.

Juliet immediately got up and turned it off. "You know we're not allowed to play CDs while we're working."

"I study better with the music on," Joe complained.

He began to work, though, and Juliet ignored him. After a while he must have grown restless, for suddenly an eraser hit the back of her head.

"What do you want?" she asked, irritated. Juliet never liked to be interrupted when she was doing anything.

"Well, you ought to know by now—" he scowled "—I need help over here."

Juliet sighed and got up from her chair. She leaned over her brother's desk and began explaining how to solve his math problem. She really didn't mind helping him. He was more inventive than she was, but he had no patience for the careful effort that went into studying subjects such as math. He also liked to read about battles, but he hated to memorize things such as spelling words.

When she finished and he understood, Joe thanked her and sighed. "You do it so easy."

"Well, you can invent things easily, and I can't do that."

Joe went back to work, but from time to time Juliet saw him glance over at her.

She hid a smile. She could almost hear him thinking: *She's up to something. She's being too quiet. I'd better keep an eye on her. One of these days she's going to get herself into trouble as sure as I'm sitting here.*

They did schoolwork all morning as usual. Then they ate a quick lunch. Afterward, Joe took off for the park to meet two of his friends and shoot baskets.

Juliet had other plans.

She got on her bike and pedaled out west of town. She turned off onto old Barber Road, for she wanted another look at the Norworthy mansion.

She knew it would not be an easy ride, and

the sun was hot. She stopped a few times and walked the bike to give her legs a rest.

Finally she came to the crest of the big hill and pushed her bicycle off to the side of the road. There she leaned it against a big pine tree so that it was hidden. And then Too Smart Jones got onto the weedy lane that led to the gray stone house.

Juliet knew very well that she was doing something not quite right. She even thought, *I suppose I wouldn't be sneaking like this if I was sure what I'm doing is OK.*

But she shrugged off that feeling and marched ahead. Everything was overgrown with high weeds and grass, but at one point she could get a good view of the house.

For some time Juliet stood just looking at the place. She saw nothing unusual, though. Then she decided to go closer and walk around to the back, staying behind bushes as much as possible. When she got there, she could hardly believe what she was seeing.

"There they are!" she whispered. "The same three cars and that black limo that I've been so puzzled about."

Since the cars were parked behind the house, they could not be seen from the road.

Even as Juliet watched, a man dressed in black came out of the house. He had his head down, so that she could not see his face. He got into the limo, he shut the door, and he started the engine. Juliet watched, wondering, as he slowly drove away.

"Well, the house may not be haunted," she murmured to herself, "but *something* funny is going on here!" She continued to watch for a while. She noticed that several of the back windows had been boarded up, but not all. By now, Juliet was just a little frightened.

"Something's going on in there," she said. "This place is supposed to be empty. Who are these people?"

Finally her curiosity got the best of her.

She noticed again that the boards over some of the first-floor windows had been removed. "Something secret is going on, and I'm going to find out what it is!"

She began to approach the house very cautiously. She kept crouching down behind bushes until she came up beneath an uncovered window. The windows of the Norworthy house were high off the ground. By standing on tiptoe she found she could barely see over the sill. But she could see.

The room she was looking into was a library. She saw several large bookshelves, filled with books. They were all brown and old looking.

Juliet shifted so that she could see the far end of the room. There, two men and a woman sat at a table. She could tell that the people were talking, but the walls were so thick that she could not hear a word anyone was saying.

They're all dressed in black, Juliet said to herself. *Everything about this old house is black! Why?* This troubled her for some reason.

Suddenly she heard the crunching of gravel. Wheeling about, she saw that a car was approaching the back of the house.

Juliet made a wild dash toward the cover of the bushes. From behind a large shrub she watched the new black car roll by. Her heart was beating so hard she thought it would jump through her sweatshirt. A car door slammed, she heard footsteps, and then the house door opened and closed.

Juliet heaved a huge sigh of relief. Then she thought, *I've got to see what's going on in there. It'll be safe enough now. They're all inside.*

She darted back to the window and peeked over the sill. She was just in time to see a man, no doubt the driver of the car, enter the library. Like a detective, Too Smart Jones made a quick mental note of the clothing he had on. And then the man suddenly turned her way. He started toward the window.

He's seen me! she thought. She ducked down below the window ledge. *Well, maybe he hasn't,* she thought desperately. *Just maybe he hasn't. But if I run, he'll see me for sure.* She held her breath as the window above her head slid open, and then something landed on Juliet's back!

She almost screamed before she realized that it was a cat. A striped cat. The cat gazed up at her and said, *"Mrow!"*

She understood now. The man had come to the window just to put the cat out. He hadn't seen her at all. *What a relief!* she thought.

The striped cat wanted to be petted, so she stroked him. But the man had left the window open, and now Juliet realized that she could hear voices.

The cat rubbed against her, begging for attention. Juliet picked him up but stayed hunkered beneath the window ledge, listening intently. She still could not make out everything that was being said—the people were too far away. But they seemed to be talking about a will. And something about court. And something about a cemetery.

After a while it sounded as if the woman was crying, and Juliet wondered, *What in the world is going on?*

She put the cat down and sneaked quickly back through the undergrowth. While she was hurrying down the lane, she took one look back at the strange house. Was that a light she saw? It was still early afternoon, but there seemed to be a light in one of the third-floor windows. And was that a sound she heard?

She stared and waited and listened, but she saw and heard nothing more.

Thoughtful, Juliet went back to where she'd left her bike by the pine tree and started to pedal toward home.

As usual, when Juliet came upon any kind of mystery, she could do nothing but think of it. The thoughts that came to her now were troubling

Once she thought, *Maybe the house really is haunted.*

But then she took a firm grip on herself. *No, that can't be. Those were real people there. There's got to be some other explanation.*

She rode slowly down the road, growing more determined by the minute to investigate the strange goings-on at the Norworthy house.

"Somebody needs to look into it," she said out loud. "Maybe the police. Who knows what's going on in there?"

Then she thought, *Maybe they're criminals, and they're making the house their hideout. Or they may be spies. Who knows who they are? But they're behaving so funny. I've got to find out why.*

A dog howled in the distance, and Too Smart Jones shivered a little. A dog's howling always sounded lonely and sad to her.

"I guess sometimes I feel like howling, too," she said. "But it would seem awfully funny for a girl to do that!"

5

The Black Fence

The field Juliet saw was full of wildflowers. They were red and yellow and purple.
The sun was bright, and a pleasant breeze carried the smell of the blossoms to her.

Now she was running through the flowers,
and Boots, her black-and-white cat, was with
her. Juliet laughed to see his four white feet leaping to keep up. From time to time she would
stop and just smell the flowers and the fresh
green grass and the earth itself. White clouds
drifted across the sky. It was a beautiful day.

Suddenly Juliet realized she had gone farther than she had intended. There, right in
front of her, stood the old Norworthy house.

Fear ran through her. She wanted to run,
but she seemed frozen in place. Then, without really meaning to, she began walking toward the house. She went up the weedy lane

toward the front porch. The mansion loomed up in front of her, shutting out the sunlight. Now dark clouds covered the skies, and a gloomy light came over the scene.

Juliet began to shiver. She looked up and saw a weird green light at the top of one of the spires.

She heard voices. Someone was coming! She wanted to run, but again she seemed nailed to the spot.

And then a long, terrifying scream sounded from somewhere inside the house. The light grew brighter and more frightening.

The front door opened, and four figures clothed in black stepped onto the porch. They started walking toward Juliet. Their eyes were hard, and their faces were like masks.

Juliet let out a scream and sat straight up in bed. Then she realized where she was. *It was just a dream,* she told herself. *Just a terrible dream.* But her hands were trembling. *It sure was scary, though.*

She sat up until her fear faded away. *I've been thinking too much about that Norworthy house just before I go to sleep. And now I've let my imagination run away with me again.*

She was ashamed to wake up her parents as she would have done if she were younger. Instead, she took her biggest stuffed toy, which was Tigger, and held it tightly. Boots had been sleeping at the foot of her bed. He meowed and climbed onto her stomach. He began clawing at Tigger.

"You're jealous, aren't you, Boots?" Juliet murmured. "Well, all right. You can sleep right here."

Juliet stroked his soft fur until the sound of purring came to her ears. She wished she could be like Boots and just be able to go to sleep without a worry. That was why people talked about "catnaps," she decided. Because cats were able to go to sleep so quickly.

She thought about praying that she would not have any more bad dreams. But she didn't feel comfortable asking the Lord for help. She thought she knew why.

"You look tired, Juliet. Are you sure you feel all right?"

Juliet glanced up at her mother, who was putting the oatmeal and toast on the table. "I feel fine, Mom," she said.

"Let me look at you." Mrs. Jones put her hand under Juliet's chin and lifted it. She felt her forehead. "You've got circles under your eyes."

"I . . . I guess I didn't sleep too well last night."

Mrs. Jones sat down and put sugar over her oatmeal and then some milk. "Aren't you hungry, either?" she asked.

"Oh, sure!" Juliet said. She quickly began

preparing her bowl of oatmeal, then took a bite. "Hot, Mom, but real good."

Her dad was gone, working. Joe was already out digging worms, for he intended a fishing expedition sooner or later.

Her mother said, "We hardly ever get a chance to talk, just the two of us. Usually Joe's here, your father's here, or we're busy with something."

"That's right, Mom."

"Then, let's talk."

"About what?"

"Anything you want to."

Juliet guessed that her mother was worried about her, but she did not want to tell Mom about the dream—or about the haunted house. "Well," she said, "let's talk about that cute green dress they've got down at Pervice's Department Store."

Mrs. Jones laughed. "I might have known you'd want to talk about something like that. You're certain you feel all right, though?"

"Really, I'm not sick. I feel fine."

Joe came in at that moment holding his hands behind his back. Juliet was not paying much attention when suddenly right in front of her nose dangled a large, moist red worm.

"*Eeeeek!* Get that thing away from me, Joe Jones!"

"This worm would go pretty good with your cereal," he teased.

"Joe, you know better than that. Take that worm out of here."

"Aw, Mom, birds eat them. Look how fat and healthy robins are. I just thought Juliet might like one."

"You heard what I said. Now, go get rid of that thing and then wash your hands."

When Juliet had finished as much of her oatmeal as she could eat, she said, "Mom, I think I'll go up and get busy doing stuff before school time. Joe might bring another worm in here."

In her upstairs room, Juliet sat on her bed. She wrote in her journal for a while, and Boots helped her by pawing at the pen as she tried to write.

"Now, Boots, I don't have time to play with you."

Boots, however, said, *"Mrow!"* and jumped at the pen, digging his claws into her hand.

"Ow, that hurt!" But she could never resist the cat for long, and she began to play with him.

Her mind was still busy with the mystery that was going on out in the country. However, she had had such a troubled night that she was sleepy. Without meaning to, Too Smart Jones lay back on her pillow and dozed off.

Juliet came awake with a start and sat up straight. Boots jumped, too. He landed with his claws on her stomach.

"Ouch!" She looked up.

There was Joe, standing beside her bed. She must have heard him come charging into her room.

"Wake up, sleepyhead! You can't sleep all day. It's time to go to school."

"Joe, what are you doing barging into my room?"

"I came to get you to go to work. You need someone to jump-start you, Juliet. You want me to carry you over to the classroom?"

"No. I can do it myself. And next time, you knock politely before you come into my room."

"Oh, I'm sorry! I didn't realize I had royalty in the family here. Yes, O Queen Juliet. I will knock and then come in bowing."

He began bowing rapidly even now, and Juliet said crossly, "You're just being silly!"

Still laughing at her, Joe turned and left.

Juliet followed him to their classroom, determining to put all thoughts of mysteries out of her mind—for now.

At noon that day, Juliet got to prepare lunch. She had learned to make delicious homemade soup. And after her mother had asked the blessing, Juliet said, "I hope you appreciate this soup, Joe. I worked hard on it."

"I think I'll be able to keep most of it down," he said with a sly look at their mother.

"What a terrible thing to say, Joe! You do

talk in such an awful way sometimes," Mrs. Jones said.

His blue eyes twinkled. "Aw, I was just kidding. It's real good soup. I don't think I could have made better soup myself with all my ability."

Juliet sniffed. "I should think not," she said. "I'd hate to eat anything that you cooked."

"Why, I can make toast, and I can open a can. What more does a guy need?"

Mrs. Jones helped herself to crackers. "I'd like to see how happy you'd be if I fed you canned soup and toast every meal."

After lunch, Juliet and Joe unlocked their bikes and went off to spend the afternoon with their friends Delores and Samuel. As soon as they reached the Del Rio house, Joe and Samuel went into the backyard and began tossing a football around.

Juliet and Delores went up to the attic. In minutes they were engaged in their favorite game—dress up. Many old dresses were stored there, some of them so old and so fragile that the girls had to be very careful with them. But it was great fun to put on the long gowns and then the strings of beads and the earrings that were kept in a small box. There were many hats to try on, too, and they played for a long time.

But at last Juliet decided that she had to

tell someone what she had been doing. "I've got something to tell you, Delores. It's about the old Norworthy place. And it's a secret."

"What is it?" Delores asked, her eyes growing big with interest. She listened as Juliet described her adventures at the house, and then she said, "A haunted house! Oh, I'd love to see it."

"Then why don't we go out there?" Juliet asked quickly. "Right now." It was what she had had in mind all the time. "It's still daytime, so it wouldn't be scary at all."

"All right. Shall we ask the boys to go?"

"No, no. We'll just go by ourselves."

It was another hot bike ride up Barber Road, and both girls were perspiring by the time they got to the weedy lane.

"We'll just leave the bikes here by the pine tree and sneak up," Juliet said. The two girls concealed their bikes and began tramping toward the old house. When they got close, Juliet exclaimed, "Why, look at that. Today there are two pickup trucks there. And workmen."

The girls crept closer but stayed hidden.

"What are they doing?" Delores asked softly.

"Looks like they're putting up some kind of fence all around the place. A big black fence."

"Why are they doing that?"

"Who knows?" Juliet said. They circled around to the back of the house, being careful to keep out of sight of the workers. Juliet didn't want to get too close, but now she was hearing something from the house that made her very curious.

"Do you hear that?"

"I hear something," Delores said. "But what is it?"

"I don't know. It's some kind of *strange* noise—like banging and scraping."

The two girls looked at each other, and Delores said, "Juliet, I'm getting scared. I want to go."

"Well, OK. Maybe that would be a good idea."

They crept back to where their bicycles were hidden and started pedaling back down Barber Road. When they stopped once to rest on the way, Delores asked, "What kind of a noise was that we were hearing?"

"I'm still not sure. Maybe somebody's locked in there and is trying to get out."

"Do you think so?" Delores cried. "Maybe we ought to tell the police."

"Not right now. Not yet."

"Why not, Juliet?"

"No, we can't tell Chief Bender until we know more."

"But maybe those people you saw dressed in black—maybe they're holding somebody for ransom. Maybe they've *kidnapped* somebody."

As a matter of fact, that was exactly what Juliet had been thinking.

When they got back to the Del Rio house, the boys met them.

"Where have you two been?" Joe asked suspiciously.

"Oh, just out riding."

"Bet you haven't," he said. "I'll bet you've been out to that Norworthy place."

Juliet was not going to lie, so she told them. Right away the two boys began asking question after question. She told them about the people in black and the weird light and the mysterious scraping and the black cars. And the fence.

Samuel said very seriously, "Next time you go out there, I want to go, too."

Juliet frowned. "I don't want our parents to hear about this—or your grandparents, either. It would just worry them a lot."

"Right," Joe said importantly. "This is just between us. Nobody will say anything to anybody else."

As they biked homeward later, Joe said, "Now, don't you go sneaking off to the haunted house again. Remember, I want to go, too."

"It's not haunted."

Joe snorted. "Well, *something* funny's going on out there."

"I know," Juliet said. "We'll have to find out what it is."

"Another mystery." He grinned. "Too Smart Jones is in action again."

"Joe, please don't tease me anymore about that."

"About what?"

"About my looking into mysteries."

"Why not?"

Juliet gave him a despairing look, but this time she only said, "I just don't like it—so please lay off, will you?"

"OK. Sure I will—for now!"

6

The Visitor

Sunday morning dawned bright, and the Joneses got up early. Sunday was always a favorite day with all of them. They liked being able to go to church and worship the Lord as a family. It was also a day when Mr. Jones could be home, and the family could spend much time together.

The usual breakfast on Sunday morning was bacon and eggs and biscuits—"real biscuits" was what Joe called them.

Mrs. Jones never bought supermarket biscuits. She always made her own and used the best of ingredients. She'd taught Juliet how to make them, too. In fact, Juliet had made the yummy biscuits they were eating right then.

Juliet's father spread butter on one and said, "You won't have any trouble catching a husband when you get old enough, Juliet. Lots of fellows would marry you just to get biscuits like this."

"Oh, Daddy, you're being silly!"

"I'm not being silly. Why, I married your mother for her biscuits. Didn't I, sweetheart?"

Mrs. Jones was used to her husband's fooling. "Yes, you did. And I married you for all your money."

Mr. Jones howled at that. "All my money— I think I had something like fifty-seven dollars when we got married."

Joe looked up from his bacon and eggs. "You couldn't do much with fifty-seven dollars, could you?"

"We couldn't, but the Lord provided all we needed. He always does. I was in school at that time, too, and I had to work nights, but those were good days."

"They were very good days," Mrs. Jones said with a smile.

"And I've loved being married to you." He grinned at Juliet and Joe. "Then you two came along, and life got even better." Then Mr. Jones looked at his watch and said, "We'd better get a move on. We don't want to be late for Sunday school."

Joe said, "I *like* to go in at the last minute. Just wait until we have sixty seconds, then go breezing in."

"I don't like doing that," Juliet disagreed. "You can't get good seats."

"We don't have to worry about getting good seats in Sunday school!" Joe protested.

They did not have to worry about getting seats in the church service either. After Sunday school they went up to the auditorium and got ready to sit about three-fourths of the way from the front. That was the Joneses' usual place.

Joe whispered, "Let's sit somewhere else today."

Mr. Jones looked down at his son. "What for?"

"We sit here every Sunday. Why can't we sit in the back over in the right corner, or up in the front right over there? Just to do something different."

"I don't see any point in that," Juliet said. "These are good seats. You're just never satisfied. You're always wanting to do something different, Joe."

"I like a little variety in my life."

"No, you don't, either," Juliet whispered back. "You like to eat the same thing every day."

Mrs. Jones hushed the argument, saying, "Just sit down!" and they sat, waiting for the service to start.

Juliet watched the auditorium fill up. She turned around now and then and looked back toward the entrance to see who was coming— and there she saw her! A tall woman dressed

67

completely in black was coming in. She even had on a black hat, and not many ladies wore hats to church anymore. And she wore a black veil over her face.

Juliet's heart began to thump. *It's her!* she thought. *That's the woman I saw at the old Norworthy place.*

"Juliet, turn around!" Mrs. Jones whispered. "It isn't polite to stare like that."

There was no choice then. Juliet turned toward the front, but she quickly realized that Joe had seen the strange woman, too. He began scribbling something on the back of the church bulletin. Then he handed it to her, but she had no chance to read it.

Their mother reached out and took the bulletin from her hand. "There'll be no note writing in church." She shook her head at them both.

Juliet sang along rather mechanically during the song service. She knew most of the songs by heart. But her thoughts were somewhere else. When the pastor got up to preach, she tried to keep her mind on what he was saying, but it was almost impossible. Too Smart Jones did not hear much of the sermon that day. All she could think of was the strange woman who had come into their church.

What is she doing here? Why is she wearing black? And why is she wearing that veil over her face? She must be hiding something!

When the service was over, Juliet could not get out of their row right away. Other people were sitting on both sides of their family, and they did not move very quickly. By the time she did get out, Juliet saw that the woman in black was gone.

I can't wait to tell Delores about this, she thought.

But this Sunday they did not go straight home. As they got into the car, her dad said, "I think we'll give ourselves a treat and eat out today. Where do you want to eat?"

"Chinese!" Joe cried.

"Barbecue!" Juliet said.

"And what do you say, Mrs. Jones?"

"I'd like to eat at Semolino's."

"That sounds good to me. You kids will have to wait on Chinese and barbecue."

So the Jones family drove to Semolino's, which was a very nice restaurant in the middle of town. They sat down at a table, and both Juliet and Joe decided to order lasagna and salad.

Juliet really liked Italian food, but she watched in dismay as Joe doused his lasagne with hot sauce. "I don't see how you *taste* anything, Joe," she said.

"I don't, either." Mr. Jones gave him an unbelieving look. "You're going to burn out your taste buds."

Mrs. Jones clucked sadly. "You couldn't possibly taste the lasagne."

"Oh, but that's where you're wrong, Mom," Joe said. "This hot sauce just brings out the flavor. Try some of it."

"No, thank you!" His mother held up both hands. "I don't want to ruin my food."

They were almost finished with the meal when Juliet happened to glance out the restaurant window. She had a forkful of lasagna halfway to her mouth, and it paused right there.

Outside, a long black limo was passing by. The same one she had seen at the Norworthy mansion.

From across the table, Joe must have seen her lift the fork toward her lips and then stop. He glanced out the window, too, and he saw the car. He kicked Juliet under the table.

She looked across at him and gave him a hard kick back. Her lips framed the words, "Be quiet."

Joe just grinned, and Juliet knew for sure that her brother would be wanting to talk when they got home.

She was not mistaken. Back at the Jones house, she went upstairs to her room. She figured that he would come up right away, and he did.

"I told you to knock before you come into my room!"

"Sorry. I forgot. Say, what about that woman in black?"

"Well, what about her?"

"She must be the same one you saw. What do you suppose she's doing coming to our church?"

"How should I know, Joe? I was as surprised to see her as you were. And why shouldn't people go to church?"

Joe tramped around her room, scowling. "There's something real funny about this. The way she's dressed with her face covered up. I think she's got to be some kind of a criminal."

Juliet thought about what she and Delores had talked about. Perhaps these people *had* kidnapped somebody and were holding him hostage.

Joe stopped pacing about and put his hands on his hips. "I know you, Juliet. You're not going to be happy until you find out who that woman is."

Boots was clawing at her shoelaces, and Juliet reached down with both hands and picked him up. She held him up to her cheek and smelled his fur. Then she said slowly, "Yes, I think I am going to look into it."

"I want to help," Joe said.

"All right, but first we've got to make a plan. Let's sit down and write everything down and see where we're going with all of this."

7

The Road Work

The church parking lot was filled with cars and vans. Excited youngsters darted to and fro while Support Group parents tried to get them organized. A babble of voices filled the air.

Joe was grumbling. "I don't see any use in wasting our time cleaning up roads."

"Well," Juliet said, "it's not a lot of fun, but it's something that needs to be done. It'll make the outside of town look better."

"Sure," Flash Gordon said. "Let's get at it." He had been cutting wheelies in his wheelchair, spinning around so fast the eye could barely follow him. "I can think of a lot of things that would be worse."

"Name one!" Joe said.

"Going to the dentist." Flash's grin showed off his white teeth.

Chili Williams's laugh rang out. "Yeah, that or taking a test at school. That would be worse."

Juliet threw herself into the game. "Or scrubbing the floor of the church gym with a toothbrush."

"Or eating spinach!"

"How about getting the measles?"

"Yeah, or getting an F in math?"

"Oh, come on, you guys! Give me a break, will you?" Joe moaned. "It just seems like such . . . such unskilled labor."

"Well, who do you think keeps the roads clean? Doctors and lawyers?" Chili waved his arms. "Somebody's got to do all this kind of work."

Juliet knew very well that Joe really did not mind doing the work. He just liked to complain. And actually, as the parents began to call out for the boys and girls to load up the cars, he suggested a way to make a game out of it.

"I'll bet I get my part of the road clean quicker than any of the rest of you."

"No, you won't!" Flash yelled. "You just watch my smoke."

All the youngsters piled into the cars and were soon on their way west and out of town. When they came to the corner of Barber Road and Water Trail, everybody got out, and their supervisor for the day, Mrs. Tanner, called

74

them together. "Here," she said, "you've all got to have on an orange vest."

"An orange vest! I look bad in orange," Helen Boyd said.

Juliet thought she didn't look particularly good in anything, but Helen always made a fuss about her clothes.

"They should have had purple for you, Helen," Samuel Del Rio teased.

"Yeah, bright purple," Jack Tanner said. He was a tall ten-year-old, thin but very athletic. "Maybe you'd look good in chartreuse."

"Chartreuse! What color's that?" Billy Rollins demanded with a scowl.

"It's a fancy color that women wear," Jack said.

"How do you know about women's clothes? You been reading those fashion magazines again?" Juliet teased.

Jack Tanner had a fair complexion, and when he blushed it was very obvious. "I don't read that junk!" he muttered.

"I'll bet you do," Billy said. "I bet you spend all your time sitting around reading girls' magazines."

"That's enough of that," Mrs. Tanner said. "Now, all of you put on these vests, and I don't want to see any of you without them. All road workers have to wear them for safety reasons. It's the law."

Juliet slipped on her orange vest and

thought it was very ugly. *Oh, well,* she told herself, *I didn't come out here to look good. I came to work.*

But Joe said, "Hey, these are cool!" He strutted back and forth in his orange vest until soon he and Billy Rollins got into a shoving match, as they often did.

Mr. Tanner came over and separated them. Then he said to everybody in a firm voice, "One group of you will go up Barber Road and the other up Water Trail."

Juliet held her breath as he assigned people to the two roads. Which road would *she* be on? When Mr. Tanner picked Juliet and Joe both for the crew on Barber Road, she doubled up her fist and quietly exclaimed, "Yes!"

The boys and girls near Juliet turned around and looked at her questioningly.

Flash Gordon asked, "So what's so exciting about Barber Road?"

"Oh, nothing," Juliet said.

But Flash rolled his wheelchair over beside Juliet, and his eyes were knowing. "You can tell Uncle Flash."

"There's nothing to tell you," Juliet insisted.

Still he looked at her with a peculiar light in his eyes. "You're withholding information, that's what," he said. "Come on, Juliet. Tell us all about it! What are you up to?"

But about that time Mr. Tanner said, "And here's your equipment, everybody." He began handing out sticks about three feet long. There was a nail in the end of each. "You can stab the trash and pick it up without bending over," he explained. "Makes work easier."

Joe squinted at his stick. "Bet I could invent something better than this!" he said. "I can invent a mini vacuum cleaner that would just suck up all this stuff."

Mr. Tanner grinned. "You do that, Joe. Next time, we'll be glad to use any inventions you come up with. But for now we'll have to stay with the old stick-and-nail routine."

"What do we put the trash in?" Jenny asked.

"You put it in these." Mrs. Tanner brought large black plastic bags out of a box. "These are leaf bags, but they're all we had. Don't try to fill them all the way to the top."

When each worker had been given a plastic bag, Mr. Tanner brought out something else. "And here are some plastic gloves. Some of this stuff may be a little messy, and these gloves will keep your hands clean."

Finally the teams were all set. Juliet, Joe, Delores, Sam, Jack, and Billy were among those going up Barber Road.

Billy, of course, could not do anything without grumbling. "I still don't see why I have to come out and do this. Why doesn't the town clean its own roads?"

"Why shouldn't we help?" Delores asked

him. "You're not too good to do some work, are you?"

Billy made a face at her and stuck out his tongue.

"Ugliest tongue I've ever seen in my life," Joe said cheerfully. "Put it back in before you scare everybody to death."

Mr. Tanner started the Water Trail crew on their cleanup. Then he came back to tell the Barber Road homeschoolers which side of the road each would be working on and where to start.

Juliet found Joe, Delores, and herself on one side. Sam, Billy, and Jack were across from them on the other side. Soon they were making a game out of it.

"I got a Hershey bar wrapper!" Joe yelled. "Let's give points. Candy bar wrappers are five points, peanut bag wrappers twenty points, any kind of printed stuff thirty points."

That was fun for a while except, as usual, the boys got into an argument over some of the items. Billy claimed thirty points when he found something from a local grocery store and Joe said that didn't count.

After a while Jack and Billy got far ahead of the others. It looked as if they were not really picking up much—just playing around.

"We could do without those two," Juliet said.

"They sure don't do much work," Samuel

remarked. He plunged his pick-up stick into an old milk carton and then deposited it in his bag. Then he said, "I don't know why people have to be so careless. It wouldn't take much effort just to keep this junk in their cars and throw it away at home."

"People just aren't very thoughtful," Juliet agreed.

They had not gone too far before Joe said he was bored. He leaned on his stick and looked at the road ahead. "You know what?" he said thoughtfully. "We're going to work our way right past the haunted house."

Sam straightened up. "You mean that old mansion is *really* haunted?"

Juliet tried to pass it over. "Oh, he's just being silly, Samuel. Don't pay any attention to him."

But Delores said, "It *is* haunted, Samuel. It really is."

"Then I *really* want to see that place!"

Juliet's crew worked their way down the road, closer and closer to the Norworthy mansion. It seemed the closer they got, the faster they worked. The sunshine was warm, but it was not terribly hot. Once in a while, Mr. Tanner would come by in his pickup. He would take their full plastic bags, toss them in the truck, and give them fresh bags.

"You're doing fine, kids," he said. "We're

going to have the cleanest roads in the United States of America."

The work went on smoothly until they almost caught up with Billy Rollins and Jack Tanner on the other side. Billy and Jack had gotten into some sort of argument and were yelling at each other.

Juliet groaned. "Listen to that. Seems like Billy can't get along with anybody."

When Mr. Tanner came by again to pick up their full trash bags, Jack came over to the truck and said, "Dad, I don't want to work with Billy anymore."

"You don't have to stay with anybody in particular, Jack. Nobody does. Fall behind or get ahead whenever you want to."

When the pickup rolled away, Billy said, "You're nothing but a daddy's boy!"

Jack was quiet for just a moment. Then he said, "To tell you the truth, I'm glad to have a dad." He looked at the pickup stopping farther down the road, and he smiled. "It's pretty nice to have a dad who does all kinds of things with you."

Billy's face fell. Juliet guessed that Billy's dad rarely did anything fun with him. He was too busy.

Then Billy looked at the bags that the others were dragging behind them. "You're nothing but garbagemen," he said. "That's what you're going to be when you grow up. Garbagemen."

Juliet and Joe, Delores and Samuel—the four of them just ignored Billy Rollins.

The work seemed to be going well. Some of the smaller boys and girls got tired and sat under a tree for a while, but Juliet and Joe and most of the others kept going.

"I feel kind of sorry for Billy," Juliet said to Joe as they each filled another bag.

"I know. You said that before. I think he's a pain!"

"I know he is, but I think he's lonesome. He doesn't have friends."

"If he wouldn't be so obnoxious, he'd have more friends."

"He just doesn't know that, though. I think he does and says awful things just to get attention from somebody."

"He gets it all right." Joe made a face. "I just don't understand the guy."

"Then Mr. Rollins—he works all the time. Billy says he leaves early in the morning and doesn't get back sometimes until late at night. Billy hardly ever sees him! He said his dad hasn't had a vacation in three years."

"Wow," Joe said. "We've had some good family vacations."

"Our family does lots of fun things together. The Rollinses are rich, but there's a lot they don't have that we have."

"Can't a guy be rich and happy at the same time? I'd like that."

Juliet laughed at him. "You're never satisfied with what you've got, Joe. I don't think you'd like being rich, though."

The truck came along again. Jack, who was in the pickup with his dad now, jumped out and threw their bags into the back.

"Are you all worn out?" Mr. Tanner asked. "Jack says he is."

"I sure am," Jack said. "This is hard work, Dad."

"Work like this will make you a better man."

"I'm not sure I want to get better that way."

Mr. Tanner grinned down at Juliet. "And it'll make you a better woman, Juliet."

"Like I always say," Joe said loudly, "hard work never hurt anybody."

Juliet made a face.

Mr. Tanner saw her, and he laughed. "I'm glad to see that one member of your family believes in hard work."

"Yeah," Jack said. "If you like work, we can put you in business, Joe. You can come over and help me cut grass after we get through here."

Joe didn't seem to care about the teasing. "At least we're almost through," he said. "Let's see if we can talk the boss here into taking us by for a hot dog after we get done."

"There's nothing like a nice nutritious hot dog after a day's hard work," Mr. Tanner said with a grin. "Let's get the rest of this trash picked up, and then the hot dogs are on me."

"How about hamburgers?" Joe asked.

"That too."

"Uh—how about steaks?"

"Don't press your luck, Joe."

"Well, just give me a hamburger *and* a hot dog, and we'll call it square!"

8

The Horrible Sight

By the time Juliet, Joe, Delores, and Sam had worked their way as far as the weedy lane of the Norworthy mansion, Mr. Tanner's truck was way up the road, picking up bags from groups that had been assigned to gather trash farther ahead.

Joe saw that and said, "You girls wait here. Sam and I are going to run up the lane and take a quick look. OK?"

"OK," Juliet said. It was only fair, she thought. She and Delores had had a private look one day. "But hurry back."

Joe and Sam walked quickly up the lane.

"There's the new fence!" Joe exclaimed. "That's some fence just to be around somebody's house!"

"Sure is," Sam said. "It could keep an elephant out."

"Why would anyone build a fence that big?" Joe wondered.

"Shall we climb over?"

"Let's walk around and see if we can find some other way to get in."

"Sounds good."

The boys walked along the fence through high weeds and past thick bushes. They did their best to keep hidden behind the brush just in case somebody was in the house. They were careful to keep well back from the fence that ran behind the mansion. And that's when Joe thought he heard something.

"Listen. Do you hear that?"

Sam listened for a moment. "It sounds like a big tractor running."

"Didn't sound like that to me."

"Wish we could see better," Sam said. "These weeds are so high back here. Looks like they never get cut."

"I think we better have a look," Joe whispered.

"Bend over, Joe, and make a table so I can stand on your back and look."

But Joe wanted to do the looking first.

Sam said loudly, "I thought of it first! And I'm more of an acrobat than you are."

"*Sssh!* OK, OK, but then I get a turn."

Joe leaned over, and Samuel, being a gymnast, jumped up with ease. Joe heard him let out a gasp of surprise. And right away Sam jumped back down. His eyes were very big.

"What's taking those boys so long?" Juliet groused. "See? Mr. Tanner's coming back this way. He'll wonder where they are."

"We'd better make this look good," Delores said. She started picking up litter, and Juliet joined her.

Both kept frantically looking up the lane. Juliet said desperately, "I wish those boys would just get back here!"

"So do I."

And here came Mr. Tanner now. He yelled out the pickup window, "Hey, Juliet, Delores. Where are the boys?"

At exactly that moment, Joe and Samuel appeared. They were stabbing at trash with their sticks as they hurried down the lane.

"Just pick up litter beside the road," Mr. Tanner called to them. "Never mind the driveways." And he drove on.

Juliet heaved a sigh of relief. "Well, they made it back just in time. I wonder what they found out."

But now here came Billy Rollins, walking back toward their starting place.

He must be quitting, Juliet thought.

Billy looked suspiciously at the four of them. "What are you up to?"

"We're cleaning the road like we're supposed to," Joe said innocently.

"You're up to something, and I want to
know what it is. We're not supposed to pick up
trash in people's lanes."

"Mr. Tanner already told us that."

Billy, however, kept asking questions until
finally Samuel said, "Why don't you give it a
rest, Billy? And why don't you do one thing in
your life without fussing about it? Don't you
get tired listening to yourself fuss?"

"I know you guys are up to something, and
I want to get in on it. Why do I always get left
out?"

"Because you make such a nuisance of
yourself, that's why," Joe growled. "Just one
time I wish you'd be nice and pleasant."

Juliet thought a hurt look swept over Billy's
face, but then his lower lip stuck out. He
looked much like a two-year-old pouting. Once
again, she found herself feeling sorry for him.

She looked at his half-filled plastic bag.
"Come on, Billy, I'll help you fill your bag.
We'll get ahead of Sam and Joe, and you and
I will pick up more trash than anybody."

"I don't need your help!" he snapped. He
turned around and stalked off.

As soon as Billy was gone, Sam turned to
the girls, his eyes bright. "You won't believe
what I saw."

"Let's not tell them," Joe said. "Let's make them guess."

"Joe Jones, you be quiet!" Juliet cried. "What did you see, Sam?"

"First, we heard this noise that sounded like maybe a tractor. So I got up on Joe's back to see."

"Yeah, and you nearly wore a hole in my shirt jumping around up there."

"But what did you see?" Juliet begged.

"Well," Sam said—and his voice grew hushed, and his eyes grew wide. He looked a little scared too. "What I saw was a backhoe."

"What's a backhoe?" Delores asked.

"Don't you know anything?" Joe said impatiently. "It's a machine that moves dirt. It looks like a big scoop shovel, and it digs big holes in the ground. My dad uses them at work."

"So what was the backhoe doing?" Juliet asked.

"That's what was a little scary," Samuel said. He swallowed hard and said nervously, "They were digging up long holes, sort of like graves. One after another."

"Yeah, and side by side."

"How do you know, Joe? You couldn't see anything."

"We took turns. I'm telling you they were digging graves with that backhoe. We *saw* them."

The girls stared horrified at Joe and Samuel.

"It couldn't be! It just couldn't be!" Juliet said.

"I know what I saw," Samuel said, "and it sure did look like graves to me."

"And that wasn't all we saw," Joe said. "While we were watching them dig those graves, we saw something else."

"What was that?"

"You remember that woman dressed all in black—the one that came to church Sunday?"

"Of course I remember her. Did you see her?"

"We sure did." Joe's head bobbed up and down. "She was in one of the windows up on the top floor."

"Yeah, and I thought I heard some screaming inside the house, too," Samuel said with a worried look. "I couldn't be sure of it with the noise of that backhoe, but it sure did sound like screaming to me."

Juliet frowned. "That doesn't sound good at all."

"Something bad is going on in that place," Delores said. "I'm sure of it."

The four trash collectors moved along, though very slowly now. When Mr. Tanner came back, he said, "You kids have got to work harder to get your section done. You don't have far to go. Right up the road there is where we'll load up. And then we'll go get those hot dogs I promised you."

90

The youngsters kept at it, and finally the last bag of trash was in the truck.

"That was a good day's work, kids," Mr. Tanner said to them all. "I'm proud of you. Your folks will be proud, too."

Like everyone else, Juliet was tired, but it was a good tiredness. She said to Delores, "It's really good to do something like this and feel like you're helping somebody. Now every time I drive along this road, it'll be nice and clean, and I'll think it's because we did a good job."

"It won't stay that way long," Billy Rollins sniffed. "Just wait. This time next week it'll be a mess again."

"Then we'll have to clean it again," Juliet said.

Billy looked at her glumly. "Who wants to spend their lives cleaning up litter?"

"Nobody," Juliet said. "But God gave us a beautiful world to live in, and we need to keep it as nice and neat as we can."

"It looks to me like lots of people don't believe that," Billy grumbled.

Juliet shook her head. "We can't help what other people do. All we can do is do our best to keep our part of it clean. It's like that song we sing at church—'Brighten the Corner Where You Are.' That's all we can do. We can't keep the whole world clean, but we can keep Barber Road clean."

"I guess so," Billy Rollins said.

Much later, after supper that night, Juliet and Joe were talking in Juliet's room. He had come down the hall and found her writing in her journal.

"I'll bet you're writing about that haunted house."

"No, I'm writing about the Norworthy house. It's not haunted."

"How do you know?"

"Because there's no such thing as ghosts haunting a house."

"OK, maybe not. But those people dressed in black—maybe they're taking dead bodies out of the house and burying them in the backyard."

"The holes they were making weren't in the backyard, were they?"

"Well, no. Actually they were quite a ways behind the house. But what difference does that make? They were graves."

"That's just wild, Joe," Juliet said. "They were probably doing something like digging a well."

"Digging a well! That's not the way you dig a well. I know how you dig a well. You bring a big truck in with a derrick on it, and you bore straight down into the earth. You don't dig a bunch of holes."

"Well, maybe it's a new kind of septic system."

Joe paused, scowling. "Well, I never thought

of that. Maybe they have to make separate compartments for the tanks now."

"Anyhow," Juliet said, "we can't solve it all tonight. Good night, Joe."

"Good night, Juliet."

Juliet got into bed and read for a long time. She was reading a series of books called Bonnets and Bugles. They were about a fourteen-year-old girl and boy who lived during the Civil War. She was on book number seven and was so interested that, by the time she noticed, it was almost ten-thirty.

"I can't finish this tonight," she said. She put the book down after marking her place and then knelt and said her prayers. After praying for her family and her friends and her church, she said, "Lord, I know there's something going on in that old house, and it makes me a little bit afraid. Please help me not to be afraid of things like this. Help us to find out what's going on and do what we should do about it—and keep us safe . . ."

She crawled into bed then, and Boots jumped up as he usually did. The cat liked to sit on her chest for a while each night, kneading her with his paws. When he stopped, Juliet said, "I sure don't know why you do that, Boots. But if you like doing it, it's all right with me."

Boots curled up at her feet then and began to purr very loudly.

Juliet looked out the window and saw the moon shining. It was round and very bright, and she thought she could see the craters on it. For a moment she thought about getting out of bed and going for the telescope, but she decided she was too tired after her busy day of work.

Almost right away, Too Smart Jones went off to sleep and had no dreams at all, which was exactly the way she liked it.

9

The Truck

At first glance, the Jones backyard seemed to be filled with boys and girls running around, but Juliet knew there were only five. Jenny, Sam, and Delores had come over. They often did this in order to study history together with Juliet and Joe. But now they were all outside, relaxing after a time with books and charts and maps.

Joe said, "I know what we can do now. We'll make up a game. Let's act out some history."

"How do we do that?" Samuel asked in a puzzled voice.

"I mean each one of us takes turns."

"Take turns doing what?"

"We'll each pick something that's happened in the world, and then we'll act it out."

"Oh, that sounds like fun!" Delores said. "But I really don't know a lot about history."

"You can think of something," Joe said. "We'll let you choose first if you want to. That way you can have the pick of everything."

Delores thought for a while. Then she said, "I'd like us to act out the story of the Pilgrims and the first Thanksgiving. I always liked that story. Could we do that one?"

"That's cool!" Joe said. "Sure."

"Sure," Juliet repeated. "We can all take different parts."

Joe looked thoughtful. "I'll be John Bradford," he said, "and, Sam, you can be the Indian chief, Squanto."

"Who will the girls be?" Delores asked him.

Joe thought some more. "You can be an Indian maiden, and Juliet and Jenny can be a couple of Pilgrim ladies."

"Do we have to write down what we're going to do?" Juliet asked.

"Nah. We know the story from school. Let's just act it out. We can make up stuff as we do it."

"What about costumes?" Delores asked. "Don't we need costumes?"

"We'll just pretend we have the right clothes on."

"Sure," Juliet said again. "We're not going to do this for an audience—just for ourselves."

The next thirty minutes were more fun than Juliet had ever had studying about the Pilgrims from a book. Squanto was supposed to talk like an Indian, and Sam had little idea of how this was done, but he did his best. The others made up their parts as they went along.

When they got to the first Thanksgiving dinner itself, Joe made up some more words. "We don't have enough to eat here for all of us and the Indians too," he said in a loud voice.

Sam—Chief Squanto—said, "I'll go out with my braves and bring back something to eat."

Sam whirled and left. At once he turned around and came right back. "We shot six deer with our bows and arrows. That ought to be plenty."

Everyone laughed. Juliet herself was laughing so hard that she could hardly say, "That's probably the quickest hunt that any Indians ever went on."

Then Joe announced, "If we don't have enough to eat, I'll run down to the grocery store and get some ice cream."

"Oh, you know they didn't have ice cream in those days, Joe!" Jenny protested.

"Well, since this is just a game, we can have any kind of food we want to. Anyhow, that's enough of the Pilgrims. It's time to act out my story now."

"Which one do you want to do?"

"I want to do the Battle of Bunker Hill."

"I knew you'd pick a war story," Juliet sniffed.

"There probably wouldn't be any America if it wasn't for Bunker Hill," Joe said loudly. "Come on now. Let's play this. You three can be the British. And Samuel and I—we'll be the Colonists."

That game went on for quite some time with a great deal of bang-bang-banging from both sides.

And then Mrs. Jones stepped out onto the back porch. She called, "I hate to interrupt your game, but it's time for your history quiz."

"Oh no, Mom," Joe moaned. "We're studying history out here!"

Mrs. Jones looked around the yard. "It looks to me like you're playing."

"Nothing wrong with making history fun, is there?" he asked, but they all headed for the door.

"You can come back out and play some more later. But right now it's time for that quiz I promised you."

The students trooped upstairs to the classroom. When they had seated themselves, Mrs. Jones began to pop questions at them. As usual, Juliet knew more than anybody else. She answered every question correctly.

Samuel groaned. "I don't know how you put all that into that little head of yours."

"My head's not little!" Juliet protested. "It's perfectly normal!"

"With all that stuff you've got in it," Sam said, "it must be crammed full."

Mrs. Jones kept them answering one question after another. But finally the quiz ended, and she gave everybody a smile. "You've all done very well. I think you deserve a reward. What would you like?"

"Ice cream!" all five yelled at the same time.

"Now, why did I think you were going to say that?" she asked, feeling in her jeans pocket. "Here's money for a treat for everybody. You go right down to the ice cream shop and see if they've got any new flavors." She handed the money to Juliet.

"Can we have double-dips, Mom?" Joe asked eagerly.

"I gave you enough for double-dips. Just bring back the change."

The ice cream shop was practically empty when they walked in.

"Can I mix up flavors, Winky?" Joe asked the server behind the counter.

Winky was the tall, skinny high school boy who worked at the ice cream shop part-time.

"Sure. You can have any two flavors you want."

"Then I'll have rocky road and black walnut."

"I'll have vanilla and chocolate," Sam said.

The girls both chose cherry nut and mint, and soon everyone was seated at a table by the window, wolfing down ice cream.

"Don't eat so fast, Joe," Juliet warned him, as she often did. "You're missing all the good taste. And besides, you're going to choke."

"Hey, I'm ten years old, and I haven't choked yet." He spooned another huge bite into his mouth and swallowed it. A nut must have gone down the wrong way, for suddenly he began coughing.

"Quick—he's choking!" Juliet yelped.

At once everyone began trying different things to help. Jenny tried to get him to drink water. Samuel jumped up and began to beat him on the back. Juliet and Delores were calling out their advice. Winky just stood behind the counter and scowled at them.

Finally Joe gave one more cough and glared around the table. "What's the matter with all of you? I'm all right."

"You nearly strangled—just as I said you would."

"That's all you know. I was just pretending."

Samuel laughed. "Sure. Sure. We know you were."

Everybody sat back down, and Joe began to eat his ice cream with more reasonable bites.

As they came to the end of their treat, Jenny said, "I wish I could have nothing but ice cream to eat every day. I never get enough ice cream—and I mean never."

"You'd get tired of it," Juliet said. "Even ice cream."

"No, not me!"

"Yes, you would," Sam argued.

"You're all wrong. I'd never get tired of ice cream!"

"Besides, the Bible says you shouldn't eat that much ice cream," Juliet said.

"Where does the Bible say anything like that?" Delores asked with a look of disbelief.

"It says someplace that we should do things in 'moderation.' That means don't eat too much of *anything*."

And then Juliet happened to glance away from the table. She let out a gasp, and her mouth dropped open.

"What's the matter?" Jenny asked. "You're not choking, too, are you?"

"Look at that. Going past." Juliet pointed out the ice cream shop's plate glass window.

The others turned and looked, too. A very large truck was rolling by. It was not the size of it, though, that had caught Juliet's attention. On the side, in big black letters, it said "Morgan's Caskets."

"Oh, I've seen that truck over at Bryant's Funeral Home lots of times," Joe said, turning back to the table.

"I have, too. But it's not going to the funeral home. It's headed the other way. Don't you think it's strange that they didn't turn and go down toward the funeral home?"

"Not strange at all," Joe argued. "Maybe they've already been there."

"But they came from the highway. They had to turn left on Elm Street to get to it, but they didn't. They turned right."

"So?" But then, after a moment of silence, Joe wrinkled up his forehead. "You're not thinking—"

"Yes, I am thinking," Juliet said. "And I'm thinking they're heading toward Barber Road."

Jenny exclaimed, "Juliet, you don't think it has something to do with that Norworthy house, do you?"

Juliet didn't have to think long. She said, "I do think so."

"What should we do?"

Juliet got up. "We'll follow it."

They scrambled outside to where their bikes were parked. Joe said, "You girls won't be able to keep up with Sam and me. But we'll try to keep 'em in sight."

"All right, Joe. We'll come as fast as we can."

The boys pedaled off furiously, and the girls did their best. But since Delores was small and not a particularly good bike rider, Juliet had to go slower for her.

"You go on and leave me," Delores panted. "I'll come by myself."

"No, I'm not going to leave you by yourself," Juliet told her. "Don't worry. The boys will see if the truck does turn into the Nor-worthy place."

Delores said, "I—I don't much like going out there, Juliet—if that's what we're going to do. I just don't like that place."

Juliet saw that Delores really looked worried. "It'll be all right," she assured her. "We won't stay long."

This did not seem to comfort Delores, but she followed as Too Smart Jones pedaled on.

10

The Plan

Well, it would have worked if I hadn't had that flat tire," Joe said.

Juliet sighed. "I know."

She and Joe were back home again. Everybody was back home again. The girls had caught up to the boys only to find that Joe's tire was flat. So that ended the chase. They didn't know if the big truck turned into the Norworthy lane or not. The two of them sat on the back step, wondering what to do next.

Boots came rubbing around Juliet's knees. Without thinking, she picked up a ball that was fastened to a rubber band and held it up.

"Here, Boots, catch this."

Boots loved that game! He batted the ball back and forth, back and forth. When he finally caught it, he growled deep in his throat.

Juliet played with the cat for a while. Then

she looked up at Joe. "This thing is *really* bothering me, Joe. I just can't seem to stop thinking about it."

"It's got me bugged, too. I'd give anything to know what's going on out at that spooky old place. I just can't figure out what in the world is happening."

"It's all so *peculiar*," Juliet said. "I wish we could just keep a twenty-four-hour surveillance on the place."

"Keep a what?"

"Oh, you know," Juliet said. "Like the police are always saying on TV. That means they watch something around the clock. It just means to watch somebody or some place all the time. But Mom and Dad would never agree to that."

"No, they sure wouldn't." Now Joe sighed. "And besides that, I imagine they wouldn't be too happy to know we're poking around that old haunted place at all."

"It's not haunted," Juliet said impatiently. "And we really haven't done anything wrong so far."

But she knew she was keeping secrets from their parents. She didn't feel comfortable doing that, for she knew deep down inside that her parents would not approve secret keeping. Also, she was pretty sure that, if she did tell them, they would tell her to just stay away from the old Norworthy house.

Juliet and Joe went down to the recreation room and played Monopoly for a while. Joe won, and he was a terrible winner. He laughed and shouted whenever he got ahead—and pouted whenever he lost.

Juliet did not particularly like board games, but it was something to do. She thought of other things as she played. Other things such as the Norworthy house.

Finally the hour grew late, and they put away the Monopoly game.

Obviously her brother knew where her mind had been, for he said, "Something will come up. You'll see."

"Sure. It always does."

"Don't worry about it."

"No, I won't."

The very next day, something did come up. It started when Delores Del Rio came by while they were playing Monopoly again. Delores invited Joe and Juliet to a sleepover at her house.

"But we won't sleep inside," Delores said. "We've got two tents, and Grandpa will set them up for us out in the yard. He said he would."

"We'll have to ask Mom and Dad," Juliet said. "They aren't home right now, but I'm sure they'll let us go. I'll call you."

After Delores went home, Joe looked

thoughtful. He said, "I think I'm beginning to get a great idea."

"You have about thirty great ideas a day, Joe." Juliet frowned at him. "With gusts up to a hundred."

"And most of my ideas are pretty good, you'll have to admit."

"OK, then, what's your great idea?"

"I'll tell you all about it later."

Juliet glared at him. "That makes me furious, Joe!"

"What makes you furious?"

"When somebody says, 'I know something, but I'm not going to tell you about it,' or, 'I know something, and I'll tell you about it tomorrow.'"

He just laughed at her. "You clean up the Monopoly game. I've got to go think about my great idea. Then I'll tell you."

Late the next afternoon, Joe and Juliet and their backpacks arrived at the Del Rio house. As often happened, Mr. Del Rio came to the door to greet them. He was a small and strongly built older man. He had been an aerialist in a circus when he was young. "Ah, my young friends," he said warmly. "Come in. I do believe my dear wife has something very special in the kitchen for you."

"Juliet's on a diet," Joe told him without smiling. "She can't eat anything but carrot sticks."

"Oh, you hush, Joe!"

But old Mr. Del Rio knew better. He chuckled and said, "I think my wife has something a little bit better than that for you."

Juliet thought that Mrs. Del Rio would probably have something *much* better than carrot sticks.

Supper that night included some wonderful Mexican food—cheese and onion enchiladas, refried beans, and spicy rice with vegetables. As they ate, Mr. Del Rio told them stories about when he and his wife were in the circus. He had some exciting tales to tell.

Dessert was fried ice cream.

"The first time you told me you made fried ice cream, Mrs. Del Rio," Juliet said, "I thought you were just joking for sure. I couldn't imagine anybody frying ice cream like it was an egg."

Actually the ice cream was placed stone-cold frozen into a crust that was then quickly baked in a very hot oven. Juliet thought it was delicious.

After the meal, the girls got up from the table, ready to help Mrs. Del Rio. That was when Joe came close to Juliet and muttered, "Now you're going to see my master plan."

"I'm not sure I trust any master plan of yours."

"You'll like this one," he promised. He turned to Mr. Del Rio and said rather loudly, "Mr. Del Rio, could I ask a big favor of you?"

109

"Anything, my boy. What is it?"

"Well, we've camped out in yards so many times, could we do something really different?"

"Ah, different! Well, I think young minds should try different things. What different thing is it that you want to do?"

"There's a nice camping place not far off Barber Road. I was wondering if we could get in your truck and go out there and put up the tents and stay out all night."

Mrs. Del Rio held up her hands. "That would be so much work!" she protested. "And so far to be by yourselves."

"Oh, Samuel and I will set up the tents. All we need is for you to sleep out there, too, Mr. Del Rio—so we have a grownup with us."

To Juliet's amazement, Delores and Sam's grandfather said at once, "I don't see what's wrong with doing that. We can take along some cookies and canteens of hot chocolate."

Joe looked triumphant. When he had a chance, he murmured to Juliet, "See? I told you something would turn up. Now you just wait and see what happens."

Juliet sent him a scowl. What did her brother have in mind? She thought she knew.

They found a clearing for their campsite just off Barber Road, and the boys had the tents up in record time. Mr. Del Rio had a camper on the back of his truck. There was a

110

mattress in it, and he said that was where he planned to sleep.

Then the old man said, "I don't know if anyone can be hungry so soon after supper, but we'll eat if you like."

"I'm *always* hungry," Joe told him.

So they ate cookies and drank hot chocolate and chased fireflies and chased each other with flashlights and just enjoyed being out in the dark until bedtime.

At last Grandfather Del Rio said, "All this is for people younger than me. I think I will go to bed." He got to his feet and started for the camper.

"Would it bother you if we played some music, Mr. Del Rio?" Joe asked. He held up his portable radio. "If we don't play it loud?"

"Not at all. It will put me to sleep."

So Mr. Del Rio went to the camper and crawled inside.

Joe turned on the radio.

Music started playing, and Juliet knew what he was doing. Now Mr. Del Rio could not hear them talking.

"As soon as he goes to sleep," Joe said quietly, "we're going to take a look at the Norworthy place."

"You mean just leave the camp?" Delores cried.

"*Ssh!* That lane's only a little ways down

the road. We can go take a look and be back in an hour."

"But what if Grandfather wakes up?"

"We'll wait until he's really asleep. And why would he look in our tents anyway? Is he a sound sleeper, by the way?"

"He sleeps like a rock." Samuel grinned. "He'll never know we're gone. And he won't hear us come back."

But Juliet was a little nervous about all this. She knew Joe often acted without thinking. She said, "I'm not sure we ought to do this. This is really sneaky. I don't like it."

"Oh, it won't take long, and we won't get real close. Look what I brought along. You haven't seen these, Sam. Or you either, Delores."

He rummaged in his backpack and brought out two objects that Juliet had seen before.

"What are *those* things?" Delores asked, puzzled.

"Night glasses. You can see in the dark with them."

"Hey, I've seen those in the movies!" Sam cried. "Do they work?"

"Do they work? Sure they work. You'll see. But we've only got two pair," Joe said, "so we'll have to take turns."

They waited while the radio softly played on. Then Samuel tiptoed over to the pickup and peered into the camper.

He came back grinning broadly. "Grandfather is snoring like a sawmill," he reported. "Like I said, he sleeps like a log."

"Then, come on. It's time for Joe Jones's master plan to go into operation," Joe said.

Juliet still felt uncomfortable. But she said to herself, *Oh, well, it can't hurt anything just to go take a look through the night glasses.*

11

The
Night Glasses

The full moon was hidden behind clouds as Juliet, Joe, Delores, and Sam tramped up the lane toward the Norworthy house.

Several times Joe said, "*Ssh!* Be quiet! Don't make so much noise!"

"You're making more noise talking," Juliet whispered, "than we are."

"No, I'm not!"

"Besides, you're breathing hard."

"I've got to breathe, don't I?" he snapped. "If you don't breathe, you die!"

Actually everybody was acting very nervous. Once a dog howled, and Juliet jumped—but then she realized that the animal was a long way off.

At last they came to the big fence that had been recently built around the property. It reared up black against the sky.

"Are we going to climb over?" Sam whispered.

"*No!*" Juliet said instantly. "We absolutely are not!"

"No, our folks really wouldn't like that," Joe agreed reluctantly.

"No," Juliet repeated.

"But we came to take a look," Sam said. "And we can't see much here. Too many trees and stuff. Let's go around to the back and find an open place."

They crept around to the rear of the house, trying hard to be quiet.

Joe said, "Now, let's try on these night goggles. Here, you take a look, Sam."

The two boys put on the night glasses and stared through them.

"I never saw anything like that before," Sam whispered.

"Me either," Joe echoed.

"Let me see! Let me see!" Juliet pulled at Joe's shirt, but he paid no attention to her.

"Joe Jones, let me see this minute!"

Without a word, he handed her his goggles. Sam gave Delores his, and soon both girls were looking toward the house.

Juliet was amazed at how much she could see with them. The outline of the house was clear. But what was *that* she saw? There were trees and bushes in the way here too, so that she could not be certain what she was seeing.

"I can't be sure . . . it can't be . . . but it looks like . . ."

At that moment, scraping sounds and a high-pitched scream sounded from somewhere in the house.

"Let's get out of here," Delores whispered. "Right now! I'm scared."

"I think that would be a good idea," Juliet said, thinking of what she thought she'd seen.

They raced through the bushes toward the front of the mansion. Nobody seemed worried about making noise this time. They were just starting down the lane when, suddenly, blinding headlights shone in from the road.

"Down!" Joe cried.

"Get over into the ditch," Juliet gasped.

All four threw themselves into the trench at the side of the lane. Juliet hugged the ground as closely as she could and kept her eyes shut, as if that would keep anyone from seeing her.

She could hear the car roaring up the weedy lane toward them. And then, to Juliet's horror, she realized that it was slowing down. She looked upward and saw that it had come to a halt not five feet from where she lay!

She was too frightened to get up and run, and she was afraid that one of the others would try to and be seen. "Lie still," she ordered in a whisper. "Don't move!"

The car paused for a moment. Juliet heard footsteps. Then there was a clanging, and the vehicle slowly started to move forward. She took in a relieved breath. The car had not stopped because anyone had seen them. The car stopped for somebody to open the gate. And when it had passed through, the gate shut with another clang.

"Now let's just get out of here," Juliet said.

"Gladly," Sam said.

"Be as quiet as you can!"

"You don't have to tell me that!"

They ran full speed down the lane and out onto Barber Road, where Delores gasped, "I'm out of breath!"

"We can't stop here!" Joe said.

"Keep going! Keep going!" Juliet urged everybody.

Back at the campsite, they all sat down panting, well away from the pickup and Grandfather Del Rio. The moon was out from behind the clouds again, and Juliet could see worry on all the faces.

"I won't sleep a wink tonight," Delores said. "I hope the rest of you didn't see what I think I saw."

"What did you all see?" Juliet asked. "I know what it *looked* like, but I wasn't sure."

Joe swallowed hard. "I don't know what the rest of you saw, but it looked to me like eight caskets for burying people—right next to those holes in the ground."

"That's what I was afraid you'd say," Juliet said.

"That's what I saw, too," Samuel said. "What's going on?"

"It's pretty plain, isn't it?" Joe nodded knowingly. "Those folks wearing black and living in that house—they're *burying* people."

"But burying who?" Delores whispered.

"We don't know," Juliet said. "But this is serious stuff."

"Did you hear that screaming and scraping?" Sam asked.

"Yes, and I've heard it before," Juliet said. "It's like they're keeping prisoners up in those steeples."

They talked for a while, and then Juliet said, "One thing's for sure, we can't let this go on any longer."

"So what do you think we ought to do? Go to the police?" Sam asked.

"I think we'll have to tell our parents first—and your grandparents—and then *they'll* maybe want to go to the police."

Sam shook his head unhappily. "Couldn't we just forget about it?"

"I'd sure like to forget it, if the rest of you would," Delores said. "I don't like the idea of having to tell my grandparents what we did."

"I don't like telling Mom and Dad, either," Juliet said soberly. "I should have had more sense than to do something I knew they wouldn't like. But telling would be the right thing, and Chief Bender is a good policeman. He'll know what to do."

Chief Bender had been police chief for a long time. He was a friendly policeman. He had even helped Juliet on some of her cases, and once she had been able to help *him*.

"I think we've been wrong about all of this," Juliet said, and she looked away into the dark woods.

"So how have we been wrong?" Joe asked.

"I mean that we should have told Mom and Dad about this funny business at the Norworthy place a long time ago. Back when it first started."

Joe acted surprised. "But we didn't really have anything to tell them a long time ago."

"That's right. They were just suspicions," Sam said.

"No," Juliet said firmly. "If I had it all to do over again, I would have gone right to Mom and Dad and told them the whole thing. I feel so bad about going without their permission. It was the same as disobeying, and Jesus says we're to obey our parents."

Joe did not say anything for quite a while after that. But when he did speak, he nodded his head in agreement. "Yeah, I guess you're right."

"I know I'm right. Every time I came out here, I had the feeling I was doing the wrong thing. I knew Mom and Dad wouldn't like it— and that's why I never told them."

Joe laughed shortly. "I did the same thing. When you've got a guilty conscience, it's funny how you don't want to let anybody know what you've done."

"It's settled, then. We'll go to our parents tomorrow morning and tell them everything."

"I still don't think we ought to tell Grandmother and Grandfather, though," Sam said. "Not yet, anyway. Let your folks handle things, and then we'll tell our grandparents later."

"All right. That's what we'll do," Juliet said. She took a deep, deep breath. "And I'm never, never, never going to keep anything from my folks again. It's just not worth it. And besides that, it's wrong."

"Me either," Joe said soberly.

Nobody was sleepy, and they sat there for a long time, talking a little and just thinking. Then they went into their tents.

Juliet and Delores lay down in their sleeping bags. It was very quiet outside. Once in a while an owl would hoot or a dog would howl far off. When Juliet did go to sleep, she did not sleep well. She knew Delores did not either, for she kept tossing and turning.

Finally Too Smart Jones began to pray, and she found that she had a lot to confess. "God, I'm so sorry that I wasn't honest with my parents. I was wrong. Please forgive me, and I promise I'll never do a thing like this again." She prayed for a long time.

12

The Surprise

Juliet and Joe arrived home at breakfast time. It was Saturday morning, and Juliet knew that their father was home for the weekend. She—and probably Joe too—dreaded going in.

"I'd rather be beat with a wet rope than tell Mom and Dad what we've been up to," Joe moaned. "Why do we do stuff like this?"

"I don't know," Juliet said. "We were just stupid."

"Well, let's go on in and take our medicine."

When they stepped inside, they found their parents just sitting down to breakfast. They both smiled a welcome.

"You're back early from your sleep over," Mom said.

Joe dropped his head, and Juliet did the same.

Mr. Jones glanced at his wife, then said, "What's wrong?"

"Dad—Mom," Juliet said, "we've got something to tell you."

Mrs. Jones's face showed alarm. "What is it, Juliet? Did someone get hurt?"

"No. It wasn't that, but it's something we've done that we shouldn't have. And we're sorry."

Mr. Jones got up from the table. "Come on into the family room, then. We can sit down there and talk."

When everyone was seated, Mr. Jones said, "You both are looking pretty down in the mouth. But I know the feeling. I had to go to my folks sometimes—and to other people too —and tell them I did something wrong. So what is it? What have you done?"

"It wasn't Joe's fault. It was mine," Juliet said. Talking desperately, she told the whole story of how she had gone more than once to the old Norworthy house.

Mr. and Mrs. Jones sat quietly, just listening, but Juliet could see the displeasure and disappointment on their faces.

Finally Juliet said, "And so last night when we got back to where we were camping out, I couldn't sleep. I've known all along I shouldn't be doing that. That you wouldn't like it. It was disobeying. I told the Lord so."

"I have to say I'm disappointed in you, Juliet

124

—and you too, Joe," Mr. Jones said. "What you did was very wrong."

"It was both wrong and dangerous," their mother said.

"I can see that now, Mom. Well, I guess I knew better at the time, but I just did it anyway. I'm so sorry."

Joe cleared his throat. "I knew better, too. And I'm sorry. I knew what was right, and I didn't do it."

"However," Mr. Jones said quietly, "I'm glad you came and told us about it. I hope you'll always come and tell us when things like this come up."

"I will, Dad," Juliet said quickly.

"Me too," Joe said.

"We're going to have to discipline both of you for this. I think you know that. You're grounded for two weeks. You're not allowed to watch television or talk over the telephone or visit your friends."

Their mother said, "And now you'd better go upstairs and try to get some sleep. You both look like you're washed out."

"I think I will," Juliet said. She looked at her parents and bit her lip. "I'm really sorry about what I did." She ran to her dad.

Her father stood and put his arms around her. "You're a good girl, Juliet. The trouble is that sometimes you just go ahead and do something before you think things through—like many other young people."

Juliet's mother gave her a hug, too, and then both of them hugged Joe.

As Juliet and Joe went up the stairs toward their rooms, he said, "I thought it would be worse."

"I did, too," Juliet admitted. "I'm so tired and dirty on the outside, but I feel better inside, now that we've talked to Mom and Dad."

Juliet showered and went to bed. She slept like a log.

"Come on down and have some lunch, you two," Mrs. Jones called down the upstairs hall.

Juliet jumped out of bed and saw that it was almost noon. She put on her jeans and a top, then a pair of sandals. She met Joe at the top of the stairs, and they went down together.

Their father was there, as he usually was for Saturday lunch. Neither parent said anything at all about what had happened. That's the kind of mom and dad they had, and Juliet was glad.

They had a good lunch, and afterward Joe went outside on some business of his own. Juliet went back up to her room and read for a long time. And then she thought about her journal.

She got out the notebook and read what she had written the day before. And suddenly a thought came to her. She slapped herself on the side of the head. "Why didn't I *see* that!" she cried aloud.

At that moment she heard her father calling her. "Juliet, come downstairs a minute."

What now? Juliet ran down to the kitchen and saw that Joe had come in and her mother was still there.

"What is it, Dad?"

Mr. Jones held a newspaper in his hand. He had an odd look on his face. "I've got something to read to you." He opened the paper and began reading an article:

> "The old Norworthy mansion on Barber Road is being restored by the great-great-granddaughter of Jebediah and Esther Norworthy. Sarah Norworthy Benson has already moved into the old family home with her husband and her two brothers. A family cemetery is being located behind the house. By reburying her parents, her grandparents, great-grandparents, and great-great-grandparents there, she will return them to their home.
>
> "In an interview, Mrs. Benson said, "My family members have been buried in cemeteries all over the country, but now we want to have them brought here and buried together.' When the restoration of the family home is completed it will be opened as—"

Juliet suddenly broke in. "They're going to open up another funeral home, aren't they?"

Mr. Jones looked at Juliet with amazement. "How in the world did you know that?"

"I just read over everything I wrote down about the Norworthy house. They put a special black fence around the place—but it isn't to keep everybody out. It's because they're funeral home people. They're always wearing these black clothes. And then we saw a big casket truck going that way. I'll bet they were delivering caskets to store away."

"Yeah, but what about all that noise we heard?" Joe asked. "That screaming sound. *People* screaming."

"What you heard was probably a circular saw," Dad said, "and not people at all. The workmen were sawing something. And when a circular saw bites into green wood, it makes a screaming sound. Sometimes when you pull nails out of old wood, that sounds kind of like a scream, too."

Joe suddenly laughed. "It would have been nice if you could have figured out this stuff, Too Smart Jones, before we got into all that trouble."

Mr. Jones himself laughed then. He gave Juliet a hug. "It's been a hard learning experience. But I suppose most boys and girls have to learn how hard it is when they keep things from their parents. I had to learn the same lesson myself."

"And so did I," their mother said with a smile.

"Aw, Mom, you never did anything wrong when you were our age."

"*Everybody* growing up does things they are sorry for. My father and mother could tell you a few stories about me."

"Hey, I'd like to hear those stories," Mr. Jones said.

"Never you mind." She smiled back at him. Then she looked over at her daughter. "Juliet, are you ever going to stop getting involved with mysteries?"

"I didn't do too well on this one, Mom," Juliet said. "But I can't make any promises."

Grinning, Joe tapped her on the shoulder with his fist. "Too Smart Jones strikes again. Tune in for the next installment of this thrilling mystery."

They all laughed, and Mr. Jones put down the newspaper. "Let's celebrate by eating out tonight."

"Chinese!" Joe and Juliet cried at the same time.

"Chinese it is, then. I can't use those chopsticks, but I do real well with a fork."

Juliet felt suddenly warm and good. She had learned a valuable lesson about being honest with her parents. Silently, she promised herself that she would never hide anything from them again.

"I think Chinese would be great. What do you think, Joe?"

"I think *any* food would be great!"

"How about snails?" she teased.

"Snails? No way!"

"You said 'anything,'" Too Smart Jones insisted.

"I meant anything *good!* Let's go for a bike ride and build up our appetites."

Get swept away in the many Gilbert Morris Adventures available from Moody Press:

"Too Smart" Jones

4025-8 Pool Party Thief
4026-6 Buried Jewels
4027-4 Disappearing Dogs
4028-2 Dangerous Woman
4029-0 Stranger in the Cave
4030-4 Cat's Secret
4031-2 Stolen Bicycle
4032-0 Wilderness Mystery
4033-9 Spooky Mansion
4034-7 Mysterious Artist

Come along for the adventures and mysteries Juliet "Too Smart" Jones always manages to find. She and her other homeschool friends solve these great adventures and learn biblical truths along the way. Ages 9-14

Seven Sleepers - The Lost Chronicles

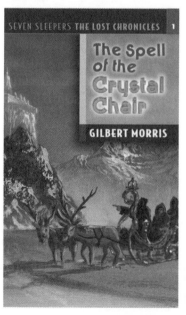

3667-6 The Spell of the Crystal Chair
3668-4 The Savage Game of Lord Zarak
3669-2 The Strange Creatures of Dr. Korbo
3670-6 City of the Cyborgs
3671-4 The Temptations of Pleasure Island
3672-2 Victims of Nimbo
3673-0 The Terrible Beast of Zor

More exciting adventures from the Seven Sleepers. As these exciting young people attempt to faithfully follow Goél, they learn important moral and spiritual lessons. Come along with them as they encounter danger, intrigue, and mystery. Ages 10-14

Dixie Morris Animal Adventures

Follow the exciting adventures of this animal lover as she learns more of God and His character through her many adventures underneath the Big Top.
Ages 9-14

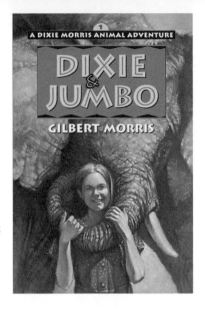

The Daystar Voyages

Join the crew of the Daystar as they traverse the wide expanse of space. Adventure and danger abound, but they learn time and again that God is truly the Master of the Universe.
Ages 10-14

MOODY
The Name You Can Trust
1-800-678-8812 www.MoodyPress.org

Seven Sleepers Series

3681-1 Flight of the Eagles
3682-X The Gates of Neptune
3683-3 The Swords of Camelot
3684-6 The Caves That Time Forgot
3685-4 Winged Riders of the Desert
3686-2 Empress of the Underworld
3687-0 Voyage of the Dolphin
3691-9 Attack of the Amazons
3692-7 Escape with the Dream Maker
3693-5 The Final Kingdom

Go with Josh and his friends as they are sent by Goél, their spiritual leader, on dangerous and challenging voyages to conquer the forces of darkness in the new world. Ages 10-14

Bonnets and Bugles Series

0911-3 Drummer Boy at Bull Run
0912-1 Yankee Belles in Dixie
0913-X The Secret of Richmond Manor
0914-8 The Soldier Boy's Discovery
0915-6 Blockade Runner
0916-4 The Gallant Boys of Gettysburg
0917-2 The Battle of Lookout Mountain
0918-0 Encounter at Cold Harbor
0919-9 Fire Over Atlanta
0920-2 Bring the Boys Home

Follow good friends Leah Carter and Jeff Majors as they experience danger, intrigue, compassion, and love in these civil war adventures. Ages 10-14

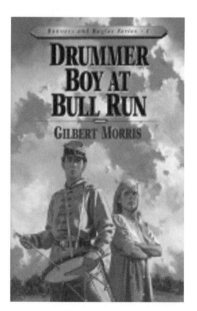